Short Fiction in

The Spectator

Short Fiction in
The Spectator

DONALD KAY

Studies in the Humanities No. 8
Literature

The University of Alabama Press
University, Alabama

Quotations from *The Spectator*, edited
by Donald F. Bond, © 1965 Oxford University
Press, are used by permission of The Clarendon
Press, Oxford, and this permission is
gratefully acknowledged.

TO

Carol McGinnis Kay
and Kenneth Curry

Acknowledgments

In common with all authors, I have received much advice and encouragement in the composition of this book. Most debts are acknowledged in the Select Bibliography, but the greatest is to Professor Benjamin Boyce of Duke University, whose essays on prose fiction in the eighteenth century are invaluable to the student and teacher of the literature of the period. His gracious encouragement in the development of this volume was most welcome.

I should also like to record my especial thanks to Professor Albert M. Lyles of Virginia Commonwealth University and to Professor Percy G. Adams of The University of Tennessee for reading the manuscript in several versions and for giving cogent criticism for its betterment.

The staffs of the libraries of The University of Alabama, The University of Tennessee Hoskins Library, and the British Museum were always very efficient and informative. My editor at The University of Alabama Press was uniformly helpful and patient, and she has saved me from numerous mistakes. But without the constant support of my wife, Professor Carol McGinnis Kay, and two summer grants from The University of Alabama Research Grants Committee this work would not have been possible.

DK

University, Alabama
November 1, 1974

Contents

Short Fiction in
The Spectator

Motto for
Spectator No. 1

Non fumum ex fulgore, sed ex fumo dare lucem
Cogitat, ut speciosa dehinc miracula promat.
—Horace, Ars Poetica, 143–44.

Not smoke after flame does he plan to give, but after smoke
the light, that then he may set forth striking and wondrous tales.

Introduction

"No Author that I know of," proclaimed Mr. Spectator in *Spectator* No. 58, "has written professedly upon it; and as for those who make any mention of it, they only treat on the Subject as it has accidentally fallen in their Way, and that too in little short Reflections, or in general declamatory Flourishes, without entering into the Bottom of the Matter."[1] He was, of course, speaking of "Wit" in terms of its eighteenth-century application, but if this taciturn literary critic and observer of the world-at-large happened abroad today, he might choose no better words to express his conclusions about the critical commentary upon a large measure of the "Wit" in the blazing success he published and presented putatively from March 1, 1711, to December 6, 1712. This neglected *corps d'esprit* is represented by the approximately one hundred pieces of fiction—short stories suggesting that brevity is indeed the soul of Wit—that are scattered throughout the 555 originally issued numbers of the *Spectator*.

Honored and avidly read in its own time, long admired, included, and mentioned prominently in the major period anthologies, the *Spectator* has always been recognized as a powerful force in the formulation and depiction of neo-Augustan manners, taste, and morals. There have been selected editions, reprints, and complete editions aplenty, culminating in 1965 with a five-volume definitive edition by Donald F. Bond, published by The Clarendon Press at Oxford.[2] Addison's and Steele's *Spectator* has yet to receive a full-length, detailed study of its contribution to, use of, and place in the short story tradition, however, and with Professor Bond's superb edition available, the time is at hand. As Benja-

min Boyce quite aptly remarked in his stimulating article survey-
ing the general characteristics of the short fiction in the eighteenth
century, "In view of the fame and quality of *The Tatler* and *The
Spectator,* one can only be surprised to discover that there is in
print no scholarly, inclusive discussion of the large quantity of
fiction in these two delightful publications."[3] The aim of this book
is to examine the short fiction in the *Spectator* and to clarify one
fundamentally important area in that large unmapped realm of
short fiction inside and outside the periodicals of eighteenth-
century England.

Naturally the subject of the short fiction in the *Spectator* has
not gone totally unnoticed by critics over twenty-six decades, but
it has by and large been only cursorily, unsystematically, or broadly pursued, evaluated, and discussed. Indeed, as early as 1711
John Gay, in *The Present State of Wit,* written from Westminster
on May 3, recognized the variety in the literary forms employed
in the *Spectator* and praised the "different manners" that were
"writ in so excellent a Stile, with so nice a Judgment, and such a
noble profusion of Wit and Humour. . . ."[4] Later in the century
Dr. Samuel Johnson in his *Life of Addison* echoed Gay's remarks
on the motley nature of Mr. Spectator's periodical: "*The Spectator*
in one of the first papers shewed the political tenets of its authors;
but a resolution was soon taken of courting general approbation
by general topicks, and subjects on which faction had produced
no diversity of sentiments; such as literature, morality, and familiar life. . . . For this purpose nothing is so proper as the frequent
publication of short papers, which we read not as study but
amusement." And Dr. Johnson soon concluded that "All these
topicks were happily varied with elegant fictions and refined allegories, and illuminated with different changes of style and felici-
ties of invention."[5] Surprisingly few critics since have gone beyond Dr. Johnson's comment about the "elegant fictions" and "feli-
cities of invention," but one who did was Thomas Babington Macaulay, who was struck by the rudimentary novelistic features in
the *Spectator.* In the July 1843 issue of the *Edinburgh Review,* he

announced, or rather, pronounced: "We have not the least doubt that, if Addison had written a novel, on an extensive plan, it would have been superior to any that we possess."[6] Macaulay's panegyric has been progressively modified in twentieth-century critical comments on the fictional devices in the *Spectator*.[7]

At the beginning of the twentieth century, in 1909, Henry Seidel Canby in *The Short Story in English* was apparently surprised to discover in the *Spectator*, and also in the *Tatler*, "the very cream of Queen Anne fiction." As he put it, "Indeed, it is astonishing to learn by investigation how much pure narrative they contain. The librarian who catalogues them under essays has fulfilled only the letter of the law."[8] This comment by Canby—who cannot be accused of having the excessive partiality of Macaulay—represents an initial, and therefore historically important, attempt to draw the *Spectator* into the tradition of the short story rather than the novel genre.[9] Although Canby's remarks are too sweeping to satisfy fully, they do cover roughly five important concerns for anyone who approaches a serious study of the short fiction in the *Spectator:* namely, the cause of the emergence of short fiction in the Queen Anne period; the materials used in such "novels," as the shorter pieces were oftentimes called; the external nature or tenor of the stories; the purpose for their inclusion in periodicals; and the problem of structure. The cause for the short story's English revitalization Canby attributes to a reaction to Restoration excesses—the short stories "in their humble way are part and parcel of that movement to picture, to study, and to reform English manners, taste, and morals. . . ."[10] The materials he notes followed several paths (the oriental tale was especially influential), but Canby follows Dr. Johnson's lead in regarding the pictures of home-bred life as being instrumental in forming the basic nature of the early eighteenth-century story: the criticism of manners and "a graceful realism."[11] Perhaps naturally he acknowledges the persuasive didactic application of the stories in the *Spectator*, but he also suggests that the new English "short story" was a result of a fusion of the *moral* and the *tale*. His extensive comment is worth quoting fully:

> And yet very little of this narrative is written for its own sake. The stories are told for what lies behind them, for the application which would be made at London tables, for the thrusts at the errors of society, by means of Lindimira, Betty Simple, the old beau, the rake, the gambler, in their pitiable or ridiculous positions. Nevertheless, these tales are no mere pendants to the essays which they illustrate and adorn. If this had been the case, such miniature fictions could never have established a narrative fashion which ran its course for a good hundred years. In them, a subtle transfusion has taken place, a mingling of the spirits of the essay and the narrative, so that, unlike their medieval parallel, the *exemplum* with its independent sermon, the stories of this Queen Anne literature embrace the essential qualities of both tale and moral.[12]

Still Canby was left with the problem of discussing structure in order to make clear the narrative's additional excellence. "It is not plot," he says. He points out what cannot be denied: the short fiction in the *Spectator* is not always technically well drawn. Often the pieces are fragmentary sketches, with few usual story elements, but with a "most delightful character limned out by suggestive word and casual acts, and growing into unforgetable likeness by the vigor, the truth, the mellowness of the conceiving, rather than by any completeness of presentation."[13] The short story in the *Spectator* to Canby was "a mixed art, part story, part character sketch, part criticism, a true art for its place and for its purposes,"[14] and for recognizing this fact at least Henry Seidel Canby made a significant contribution to *Spectator* criticism. We now need to define "its place" and "its purposes" more precisely and to reexamine the generalizations he offered as truth.

One of the latest inclusive analytical remarks regarding the *Spectator*'s use of fictional techniques appears in Donald F. Bond's introduction to his five-volume 1965 edition of the *Spectator*. He agrees that the short story is an integral part of Addison's technique of combining a thoughtful analysis with a neat and graphic incident. "Two of his best treatments of courtship and married life," says Professor Bond, for example, "are characteristically presented as imaginative tales—the modern women of Hensberg (499) and the auction of women (511)" (*Spectator*, I, lx). About Steele's contributions, Bond flatly states that some of his best papers are in the tradition of La Bruyère's characters. Bond is writing an introduction, and the nature of his task forces him to list rather than analyze many of the stories in which he sees particular merit, but as a judicious scholar of the *Spectator* his opinions demand closer examination of the text. For example, after listing a number of Addison's enlivening real or imaginary tales, he sums up Addison's efforts in this manner:

> Above all, of course, there are the essays portraying Sir Roger de Coverley, at home (106, 107, 110, 112, 122, 131) and in London (269, 329, 335, 383), together with the fine papers on his death (517), on Will Honeycomb's marriage (530), and Sir Andrew Freeport's disposal of his own estate (549), which represent perhaps the finest achievement in English fiction before Richardson. (*Spectator*, I, lxi)

Such a generous comment by Professor Bond reflects the gradual, growing awareness over the years of the significance and the quality of the prose fiction in the *Spectator* as well as indicates the need to go deeper, to delve longer, and to analyze and classify the prose fiction systematically.

The subject of the short fiction in the *Spectator* has not lacked many general and valid remarks; nevertheless, there is a very real need to remedy the lack of incisive and thorough examination that Robert D. Mayo remarked in *The English Novel in the Magazines, 1740–1815*: "Except for mention of Sir Roger de Coverley, the oriental tales of the *Rambler* and *Adventurer*, Smollett's *Sir Launcelot Greaves*, and Goldsmith's *Citizen of the World*, most literary historians have been content to let periodical literature before *Blackwood's* go by the board."[15] The fiction in the *Specta-*

tor—which almost always has the single action, the unity of mood, and the strict limitation of characters that denote a short story—has all too frequently been seen simply as a "reaction" to those mysterious "Restoration excesses" or as a "forerunner" to the novel.

But what is a short story? The modern word "story" comes from the old French *estoire* and the Latin *historia,* or history, and essentially the short story is seen as a retelling of something that happened, whether pretended or actual.[16] Frank O'Connor recently stated that the distinguishing difference between the short story and the novel was not the length, but rather the "difference between pure and applied storytelling. . . ."[17] This "pure" storytelling that is the short story may then be defined very broadly for the purposes of this investigation into the nature of the short fiction in the *Spectator.* From the plethora of possibilities the basic description of Lionel Stevenson is outstanding: "The short story has a single action, with unity of mood and strict limitation of characters."[18]

In this study the prose fiction in the *Spectator* is approached in both a historical and critical manner. The title I have adopted—"short fiction in *The Spectator*"—assumes as a matter of course an aesthetic over and above a strictly historical approach to the subject. Much of the fiction in the *Spectator* arises from a single incident, which is full of suggestion; most of the stories are short by nature and not simply condensed, and they are normally told in a single scene. Concerning length, Benjamin Boyce's comments are noteworthy: "Distinctions of length in eighteenth-century fiction are, at the lower end of the range, not usually significant for quality, method, or style. . . . One of the fortunate circumstances in this period of development in prose fiction was that in the realm of story-telling there were few generally recognized rules and no undisputed models, ancient or modern."[19] If the term "short story" can be used to mean what it says, no difficulty arises in applying it to the *Spectator*'s "striking and wondrous tales," a selection of fiction with considerable variety of form. This variety in story types in the *Spectator* was a deliberate attempt to please the diverse reading audience, for the situation Mr. Spectator faced as editor is made clear by the motto attached to No. 92: "It is much like guests who disagree; their tastes vary, and they call for widely different dishes. What am I to put before them? what not?" (Horace, *Epistles*, 2.2.61-63).

Those dishes of daily entertainment and instruction that Addison and Steele began serving an appreciative public two months after the *Tatler* stopped were quite markedly planned to capture the readers' imagination and to keep them coming back for more. "In a word," Mr. Spectator notes in No. 179, "the Reader sits down to my Entertainment without knowing his Bill of Fare, and has therefore at least the Pleasure of hoping there may be a Dish to his Palate" (*Spectator*, II, 204–05). The variety of subject matter and treatment in the first few numbers—incorporating the establishment of the narrative frame and including an allegory, criticism of opera, and an essay appealing for the attention of the feminine reader—reflects the announced purpose of the authors to broaden the minds of a wide range of Englishmen. Naturally the device of the frame, with Mr. Spectator as a putative author who may relate episodes, participate in events, and include letters from correspondents, increases the possibilities of effecting variety smoothly. This "Licence allowable to a feigned Character" accounts in large measure for the numerous kinds of fictional narratives and story types in the *Spectator*. The variety of form is the chosen way to "represent Human Nature in all its changeable Colours" (*Spectator*, IV, 492; *Spectator*, II, 450).

The 555 issues of the original *Spectator* are comprised of three groups: 100 papers deal exclusively with serious, often philosophic or critical, matters of a rather specific nature that support a stated proposition; 191 papers contain material with a far looser construction and present much fiction, ranging from a paragraph to five thousand words in length; the other 264 issues are predominantly made up of letters from correspondents, and these, too, sometimes contain stories or narrative material of a fictional

or semifictional nature. Mr. Spectator, a believable character as
well as a mask for an individual author, does not make his individual presence felt in the essays of the first group, which contains such essays as the criticism of *Paradise Lost*. Wherever Mr.
Spectator assumes the role of both narrator and character, however, the writing always is presented from a fictional point of
view.[20] The group composed of letters from various correspondents further expands the fictional point of view in a large number of instances, and the authors, speaking in the first person,
serve much the same function as Mr. Spectator.

Although the *Spectator* contains many types of stories—either
in summary form or more fully developed—nearly all of them have
one characteristic in common: an obvious moral. This practice follows in the tradition of the *Gesta Romanorum*, which added to
each tale a moral in which some precept is induced from the incidents. This same moral purpose was evident in such Renaissance
works of fiction in England as Pettie's *A Petite Palace of Pettie
His Pleasure* (1576), which stated the moral purpose to cover up
what many consider lewd tales.[21] Perhaps still closer to the *Spectator's* moral purpose was John Lyly's *Euphues*, with its avowed
desire to study human psychology and to set up models for the
improvement of both manners and morals. Lionel Stevenson says
that "Lyly was one of the first writers to realize that fiction can
exert a social influence because it illustrates precepts in action instead of merely stating them in general terms."[22] Addison and
Steele, too, were aware of the power of fiction to "exert a social
influence," but apparently they were equally cognizant of the fact
that a variety of forms would be needed to keep the attention of
an audience accustomed to didactic appeals. The variety that
John Dunton offered his readers in the *Athenian Mercury* or Peter
Motteux his in the *Gentleman's Journal* certainly did not go unnoticed by Addison and Steele.

The ingenuity and flexibility of the narrative methods used in
the *Spectator* often seem to defy strict, absolute, and final classification, but there are certain types or forms into which most of

the stories fit. Among these types are: (1) the Character, (2) the dream vision-cum-allegory, (3) the fable, (4) the domestic apologue, (5) the satirical adventure tale, (6) the oriental tale and rogue literature, (7) the fabliau, (8) the exemplum, and (9) the mock-sentimental tale. In each grouping there is, of course, some overlapping, but every effort has been made to place a story into its most specific mould and to supply cross references in significant instances. Such a detailed description and classification of the narrative elements and devices and types of stories in the *Spectator* should, and I certainly hope will, prove useful to readers and students of the *Spectator*. Concerning Steele's *Tatler*, Robert Mayo maintains that the "narrative devices, in particular, deserve a close scrutiny, since they were to become the basic coinage of magazine fiction for the next hundred years."[23] This statement applies just as well to the *Spectator*.

I

The Storytelling Tradition and Periodical Antecedents to The Spectator

The mind ought sometimes to be diverted, that it may return to thinking the better.

—Phaedrus, *Fables*, 3.14.12–13
Motto for *Spectator* No. 102

The short story as we know it, a species of fiction distinct in purpose and in method from the novel, a popular and respected genre in its own right, dates only from the nineteenth century. Yet there is perhaps no kind of literature that the expression "not for an age, but for all time" more appropriately fits. Back from Poe's Baltimore, Hawthorne's Concord, and Mr. Spectator's London, its roots stretch across centuries and pass over barriers of language and temperament in a multiplicity of entanglements that lead to the shores of ancient Milesia and to the pages of the Bible, to Greece, to Rome, to France.[1] Since the discovery of fire, man has consistently diverted his mind and rejuvenated his spirit by spinning tales and relating stories, and many of these stories have had an unaccountably rapid transition from one country to another.[2] At once it is apparent that the *Spectator* strikingly reveals this relentless transition of common story material from country to country and from age to age, for it makes extensive use of story materials from another time and place. It cannot be emphasized too strongly, however, that the *Spectator* is a product of its own time—it has been called a typically eighteenth-century tour de force—and therefore one must constantly be aware of the "backgrounds" preparatory to the appearance and splendid success of such a periodical. There was something called short fiction in the seventeenth century.[3] There *were* short "novels" in periodicals before the *Tatler* and the *Spectator*. Most importantly, a general survey of English periodical fiction from 1690 to 1710 is essential to clarify the place the *Spectator* has in the steady advance of prose fiction in the eighteenth century.

England had seen "short stories" in verse in the works of Chaucer, especially, and Gower, whose *Confessio Amantis* (1382 or 1384) was actually a collection of short stories in verse exemplifying ethics and doctrine. The years between Chaucer and the Elizabethans, however, saw little advance in the use or art of the short story even though the *Gesta Romanorum*[4] was translated from the Latin. In 1576 George Pettie's *A Petite Palace of Pettie His Pleasure* was published, and it consisted of twelve tales whose plots had been drawn largely from classical and Latin sources.[5] Lyly's *Euphues* furthered the cause of prose fiction two years later. Even so, the late 1500's and early 1600's was a time for the theatre, and the short story, and fiction generally, made little apparent headway in the face of the puritanism of the 1640's and 1650's. *Apparent* is the right word because there were developments that were later to become more noticeable, and these developments occurred in the application of Bacon's new inductive methods into human behavior in such works as Robert Burton's *Anatomy of Melancholy,* Joseph Hall's *Characters of Virtues and Vices,* Sir Thomas Overbury's *Witty Characters and Conceited News,* John Earle's *Microcosmography,* and Thomas Fuller's *The Holy State and The Profane State.* The short prose narrative, called the *novel* in the continental fashion until much later, survived, though relatively unnoticed, through the blaze of Restoration drama.

Nevertheless, as Charles C. Mish points out, "if the seventeenth century has no Sidney or Greene or Lodge it does have a number of interesting and highly readable volumes of fiction which can easily challenge comparison with their sixteenth-century predecessors."[6] A wide variety of types was available, "ranging in length from the huge romance in the French manner to pithy anecdotes, in tone from the courtly to the everyday, and in style from plain down-to-earth raciness to impossibly high-flown estheticism."[7] Most of the fiction in the seventeenth century was either romantic or realistic. Romantic tales, often reprints of older stories, proved very popular, especially Lodge's *Rosalynde,* Greene's *Ciceronis Amor, Pandosta, Never Too Late (Francesco's Fortunes),* and *Menaphon,* Hart's *Alexto and Angelica* (1640), and John Reynolds's *Flower of Fidelity* (1650). Realism appeared increasingly in antiromances such as the anonymous *Westward for Smelts* (1620) and in jestbooks and jest-biographies, which "attempt to organize their narrations of incident around the life of a single well-known individual, of whom they offer a sort of life-story."[8] In some miscellaneous fiction of the century the narrative element shares the limelight with the didactic, as in the *Spectator,* and this fiction is represented by Lucian's *True History* (translated into English in 1634), Bacon's *New Atlantis* (1626), and Joseph Hall's *Discovery of a New World* (c. 1609). Satire, in such works as John Johnson's *Academy of Love* (1641), also contributed to the progression of prose fiction even though the narrative thread is often weak. Robert Burton, furthermore, in his hortatory books *Wonderful Prodigies of Judgment and Mercy* (1681), *Unparalleled Varieties* (1683), and *Female Excellency* (1688) made excellent use of short prose illustrative anecdotes to point up his precepts (in much the same way Mr. Spectator was to employ thirty years later). Charles C. Mish correctly and succinctly states the general truth that the seventeenth century assuredly did possess writers "who could tell a story, who could write dialogue, and who were interested in the analysis of feelings."[9] The clear outline of prose fiction at the dawn of the eighteenth century is evident from what William Congreve wrote in the preface to *Incognita* in 1692:

> Novels are of a more familiar nature; Come near us, and represent to us Intrigues in practice, delight us with Accidents and odd Events, but not such as are wholly unusual or unprecedented, such which not being so distant from our Belief bring also the pleasure nearer us. Romances give more of Wonder, Novels more Delight.[10]

The mélange of short prose narratives that appeared in the *Spectator* was still, however, a long step from Congreve's *Incognita*. On the other hand, it is an easy step and infinitely simpler to appreciate the nature (and indeed the presence) of this fiction if it is viewed with a knowledge of the fiction and quasi-fiction that, for two decades before the *Spectator,* had been finding its way with increased frequency—by fits and starts—into the fledgling periodicals of the era. "The moral emphasis of Dunton and De la Crose, the erudition of Oldenburg and Hooke, the wit of New [*sic*] Ward and Defoe, the miscellanous entertainment of Motteux"—all these qualities, remarks Walter Graham in *The Beginnings of English Literary Periodicals,*[11] appear, greatly transformed, in the *Spectator.* It is therefore beneficial to survey the fiction in selected periodicals[12] from 1690 to 1710 in order to place the fiction of the *Spectator* more precisely in the perspective of current trends that it and the *Tatler* not only reflected but also crystalized and made tremendously popular.

Generally the periodicals of the years 1690–1710 have two purposes: to instruct or to entertain and to do both as far as possible. The fiction to a large degree demonstrates the same concerns as the fading Restoration drama, but at the same time several periodicals reflect King William III's concern with a new code of morality in their numerous "cases" and questions-and-answers, which happened as often as not to be entertaining as well as instructive. Such works as La Crose's *Works of the Learned* (1691–92) and John Dunton's *Compleat Library* (1692–94) were addressed to a particular audience, which wanted to be instructed by abstracts of new books of an historical, antiquarian, or scientific nature. All these abstract journals were suspicious of "Plays, Satyrs, Romances, and the like," but simultaneously fiction was being printed regularly in the *Gentleman's Journal* and fact was being fictionalized in the *Athenian Mercury*. One abstract journal, the two-page folio half-sheet *Mercurius Eruditorum,* which began August 5, 1691, discussed books and authors but did so in dialogue—an interesting instruct-as-you-delight format in which the characters "Alexis, Philemon, and Theodore" meet weekly to "discuss" the books they had read. This was, to be sure, a clear anticipation of the "club" idea that the *Spectator* employed later.[13] The important point is that fiction, although looked upon with contempt by "men of sense," nevertheless made progress, perhaps accidentally, in even such endeavors as the *Mercurius Eruditorum.* The time was one in which audiences were ill defined, where periodicals were often either narrowly focused or extremely broad in scope. There was a hit-or-miss nature to many of the efforts, and some stopped with the same issue as they began, but by 1709 short fiction, still dubious and generally unfamiliar as a form of entertainment, was able to play an important role in the success of the *Tatler.*[14]

John Dunton's semiweekly *Athenian Mercury* (March 17, 1691– June 14, 1697) has a small but secure position in the magazine tradition in prose fiction.[15] This periodical represents a definite shift toward the common, miscellaneous reading audience; its purpose was expressly to communicate knowledge "more generally and easily than has been formerly done." Furthermore, its fictionalization of "facts" helped to prove that "novels" could, in the future, be adapted to realism for instructional purposes. The last benefit was, admittedly, a happy by-product for the periodical short story, because Dunton's fundamental purpose was quite serious. He aimed to answer

. . . *all manner* of Nice and Curious Questions in *Divinity,*

Physick, Law, Philosophy, History, Trade, Mathematick, &c. and all other Questions whatever proposed by *Either SEX,* or in any Language, fit for a Resolution.[16]

There was no formal fiction in the *Athenian Mercury.* But in answer to the numerous questions and representative "cases" that came in from the public for an answer or a comment concerning conduct, the editor wrote replies laced with homilies in everyday language. It is naturally not clear how many of the "cases" were invented, but it is safe to suppose that many were fictional. In the first volume, for example, a writer wishes to know "whether there ever was such a thing as change in sexes," and in the answer three "cases"—in which we learn something about the place, name, situation, and action involved—are presented to show that the answer is "yes."[17] Another writer relates an anecdote about a little sick girl, who has something hung around her neck, which is opened when she recovers, revealing the words "Devil made her well, and take her into hell." The little girl gets sick again.[18] While thoroughly unsophisticated, these two examples (each about 100–150 words long) illustrate the realistic, contemporary flavor of some of the questions and answers that have a definite narrative tendency.

All the "cases" purport to be true, and a few, such as the account of the six nights' rambles of a young gentleman,[19] are clearly satirical. Dunton seldom missed a chance to reinforce the moral or to chide misconduct, and the "cases" never quite overthrow their utilitarian yoke. In the *Athenian Oracle* (1703–10), which was mainly a reprint, partly a continuation of the *Mercury,* the following "case"—no different from many in the *Mercury* itself— shows how Dunton's periodicals anticipated the middle-class world of *Mrs. Veal* and *Moll Flanders:*[20]

> *Q.* A young woman, who 'tis not questioned is in the main chaste enough, yet being unmarried, gives great encouragement to a man who is married to a cross ugly old woman that he hates, and whom he does not dwell with, though he allows

her a handsome maintenance; she keeps him company, receives presents from him, and it's strongly presumed he promises her marriage when his old woman dies, and will, no doubt, never attempt her chastity, or do anything knowingly to lessen her reputation. It's believed they love one another so much, that they are so blinded as not to think their keeping company, though known to many, is scandalous, or that they are laugh'd at for it.[21]

Now, demands the correspondent, "Pray for judgement as to the honesty of the matter, and how their friends may awake them out of this stupidity?" Whereupon, the *Athenian* in a typically high-handed manner declares that it was neither prudent nor honest. This element of contemporaneity prompted Robert D. Mayo to remark that the *Athenian Mercury* "employs to a very striking degree those basic methods of the new fiction which Ian Watt embraces in the term 'Formal Realism,' and which Defoe is often credited with inventing."[22]

Following the *Athenian Mercury* by only nine months, the monthly *Gentleman's Journal* (January 1692–November 1694) went beyond the infantile narrative qualities exhibited in the *Mercury* and introduced genuine magazine fiction to the English audience. Peter Anthony Motteux, who had come to England from France seven years earlier and admittedly was influenced by the *Mercure Galant*,[23] devoted several pages of each issue to "novels," or 1400 to 2000 word short stories, ranging from adventure stories to allegories, from satire to love intrigues that Restoration playwrights might have envied. A variety of types of prose fiction, as well as poetry, criticism, letters, essays, and reviews, helped Motteux attract a broad spectrum of readers nineteen years before the *Spectator*. In the thirty-one short stories that appeared in the *Gentleman's Journal* the variety of subject matter and development certainly reflects the range of the shorter fiction of the time. Action and situation are more important than either character or setting; extravagant romance is severely tempered by a trend toward contemporary life and characters that points directly to Sir Roger de Coverley and his exploits.

In contrast to Dunton's *Mercury*, Motteux's primary purpose, as revealed in the dedication to the Earl of Devonshire, was to divert and "to disingage your Thoughts from the daily pressure of Business."[24] This is not to suggest, however, that the stories are totally devoid of a "moral lesson." In fact, one of the techniques employed by Motteux anticipates Addison's famous dictum about instructing and delighting at once. Motteux might just as well have been guided by the same motto selected by Mr. Spectator for *Spectator* No. 102: "The mind ought sometimes to be diverted, that it may return to thinking the better." For example, in the first number the author of "The Noble Statuary," like Mr. Spectator, uses a story to illustrate a point that he makes at the beginning.[25] He opens with specific remarks about grieving widows and grief in general, and he postulates that sometimes veils that hide inward dispositions "serve only to give silent invitation into the Inn to the gazing Passenger." In support of this generalization, he tells the story of a knight who dies, leaving a beautiful wife. A stone-cutter for the monument, who is vividly described as a boon companion, arrives at the widow's house and woos her. Later, at the tavern, he talks too much, it gets back to her, and thereafter she refuses his suit. The story transcends mere divertissement when the omniscient narrator interrupts at the conclusion to speak seriously and directly to the reader: "no, he was not the Man you take him." That Motteux consciously recognized that the "novel" might be instructive, and amusing at the same time, is made clear in the very next issue: "Poetry will but inflame their [my children's] blood, and Novels teach them to cool it"[26] Likewise, the author of "A Love Story" comments after the story, "I need not tell you that this is a very true Story, there are but too many of both Sexes that easily make the Application of it if they please."[27]

The subject matter of some of the stories in the *Gentleman's Journal* is similar to that of tales related in the *Spectator*. Most of the stories are satirical adventures where intrigue is thick and

artistic merit is thin, but there is abundant sensibility in the handling of love themes, which reminds one of Steele's sentimental
love yarns. In one place the story is related of a woman who
wants intellectual love only and lives for three years on a platonic
level with a man whom she decides to marry—but he does not
desire it, and she dies.[28] In another place "Love Sacrific'd to Hon-
or" reveals the same quality, as the following summary suggests:

> Trueman and Sparkly, with good estates, are intimate acquaint-
> ances, if not friends. Trueman will not go to visit his beloved
> Theodosia without Sparkly's going along, too. When Trueman's
> father dies, however, he goes to the country and asks Sparkly
> to "sollicit his suit" with his mistress Theodosia in his absence.
> Sparkly agrees, promptly falls in love with her, and they become
> fond lovers. After two years, Trueman returns as heir to the
> estate, and finds out that Sparkly and Theodosia have broken
> up before their intended marriage. Still loving Theodosia, True-
> man seeks to avenge her honor and forces Sparkly to marry her
> —thus sacrificing his love for her honor.[29]

Other such sentimental stories are "The Poisoned Lover,"[30] "The
Lover's Legacy,"[31] and "The Treacherous Guardian."[32]

Another resemblance between the subject matter of the magazine stories in the *Gentleman's Journal* and the *Spectator* is ap-
parent in the allegories. The best example is the one entitled "The
Birth of Love and Friendship," which relates the life history of
Beauty and Goodness, who are neighbors, and tells of the mar-
riage of Beauty and Desire and the birth of their offspring, Love.
This story is closely akin to the story of False Wit in the *Specta-
tor*. This final category of comparison helps to reinforce Robert
Wiedner's analysis of the significant effect of the *Gentleman's
Journal* on later miscellanies and periodicals. In his view

> Twenty years before the *Spectator*, the *Gentleman's Journal*, an
> enticing microcosm, reveals in its often spicy chronicles a spirit
> of ardent research that is blossoming and maturing. The nascent
> journalism will certainly be further refined, but with Motteux
> one already sees the active part that he will henceforth take in

the intellectual life of the nation. For he claims justly to make himself the mirror of the best part of the country, of that class which—without its always having the clearest awareness of it—represents in the eyes of the historians the best of the national soul.[33]

When Ned Ward's *London Spy* began its eighteen-month run in November 1698, the moral climate had changed somewhat: William III had in 1698 issued a proclamation against all forms of vice and impiety, and moral reform was becoming fashionable.[34] Still, the *London Spy* is lively and amusing throughout, much more specifically satirical in its exaggerated but realistic portrayal of Englishmen than the *Gentleman's Journal,* and the description of the London life is related "with such gusto that one may be pardoned for sometimes doubting the sincerity of his strictures upon those whom he scourges."[35] A firm believer or not, he was successful sometimes in being allegorical in the moral manner of Addison and Steele.[36] In addition, the *London Spy's* presentation of a country gentleman being shown around London by a city acquaintance is a notable anticipation (though not, of course, the only one) of Sir Roger de Coverley. Dialogue between the two, however, unlike that in the *Spectator,* is merely a device to present two viewpoints and contains no convincing give-and-take between two believable characters.

Incorporated within the narrative framework of the *London Spy* are several short stories that are used for didactic and entertainment reasons. In No. 3 Ward interweaves the illustrative story, told by the city acquaintance, of a man who rose in London by honesty and industry, simply by buying a broomstick, sweeping the wharf of a stranger (thus gaining a friend), and becoming eventually an estate-owner—by work! An amusing anecdote is related in No. 5 when the two friends pass the lame hospital, which always has had distemper in it because the bitter sister of a rich donor has put a spell on it. Later, when they go to a Turkish bath (No. 9), the rubber tells a story that Ward introduces in the manner of Addison: "And that the reader may be a partaker of our mirth, I have here made a recital of one of his comedies, in which he himself was the principal actor." The story concerns an hilarious debtor-snapper who is brought unawares into the bath, where the attendants pretend to be devils punishing him in hell. When he runs disrobed into the streets, people think he is mad. In the course of the following months, several other stories, mostly didactic, are included—two in No. 13 when the Tower Hill servant, who is very fond of stories, is portrayed.

The Characters in the *London Spy* are numerous and provide still another parallel to the kind of material found in the *Spectator*. Generally the Characters are made vivid and realistic to the contemporary Englishman; in No. 6 the Character of the horse-mountebank is made "a true portraiture" by reporting the language and mode of talk of the man. A number of the Characters are not so specific in reference. The ones of the Irishman (No. 16), the Beau (No. 16), a reforming constable (No. 15) are examples of this type, and perhaps the Character of "A Modern Critic" is the most interesting. It begins in this manner:

A MODERN CRITIC

Is a compound of some learning, little judgment, less wit, much conceit, and abundance of ill-nature. Wanting true merit, he aims to raise a reputation not by his own performances, but by others' failing. These he takes more pleasure to expose than he does to mend, and he reads an author as much in search of his faults as a wise man does for his knowledge.

"Whenever he repeats any grave verse," Ward goes on to say, "he has more turns in his voice and changes in his countenance than a young preacher in his sermon upon Death and Judgment."[37]

Continuing in the steps of the *London Spy* in its efforts to amuse the general periodical audience in a "wholesome" manner was the *Weekly Entertainer,* of which unfortunately only the October 24, 1700, number has been preserved. It is, in spite of this, an important antecedent to the *Spectator* in form and content. It was a large half-sheet folio and contained a single essay. That essay was actually a piece of short prose fiction, a dream narrative, which Walter Graham found "not greatly different from those of Steele and Addison."[38] It had, furthermore, a definite, if not obtrusive, reforming aim.

Surprisingly, a few fictional methods employed in John Tutchin's *Observator* (April 1, 1702–12) are reflected in the *Spectator*. The periodical was ostensibly wholly political in nature and reported a great deal of anti-Jacobite news; but when news was short, or when the Queen's title to the Crown appeared especially safé, Tutchin printed a few short stories in the dialogue fashion that became the format after June 24, 1702. "A Story of Jessamy Tom" shows the same concern with contemporary characters and realistic events that has been noted in the *London Spy*.[39] The dialogue between a countryman and the observator immediately leads to another story, and it is apparent that the stories serve to illustrate points or questions raised. Moreover, in the same issue (April 1, 1704) another device used by Mr. Spectator appears— the first-person story of a reader that is related in the form of a letter. The use of realistic, contemporary plots and characters, the use of stories to support points, and the letter-story—all these aspects of short prose fiction Mr. Spectator employed, too.[40]

Women's journals offer two outstanding examples of interest in short prose fiction. In 1704 John Tipper's *Ladies' Diary,* a miscellany in the style of the *Gentleman's Journal,* contained short stories, and the response to his call for reader submissions was so great "from all Parts of the Kingdom" that he declared he could not "insert a Tenth Part" of what he received.[41] *The Records of Love, or Weekly Amusements for the Fair* (1710), another miscellany, also emphasized prose fiction and love, but it too favored virtue and propriety, and it placed sentimentality above satirical subjects—as did Steele.[42]

The most important antecedent to the *Spectator,* of course, is the *Tatler,* and it is clear that in the use of fiction the *Tatler* was to do much to cultivate a taste for fiction, which was still con-

sidered by many readers "a dubious, trivial, or at best an unfamiliar form of entertainment."[43] The fact that the prose fiction
in the *Tatler* was unquestionably an important factor in its success has recently been carefully explored by Professor Richmond
P. Bond in his admirable book *The Tatler: The Making of a Literary Periodical* (Cambridge, Mass.: Harvard University Press,
1971), where he demonstrates that the fiction in the *Tatler* represents not so much a continuing familiar popular tradition as it
points to the birth of a new one, which combines the essay, the
Character, the letter, and a series of narratives in an imaginative
creative evolution of a different sort of story.[44]

The *Tatler* contains a large number of fictional and semifictional pieces, some of which, in the manner of the *Gentleman's Journal* and *Records of Love*, are given formal titles such as "The
Civil Husband" (No. 53), "The History of Tom Varnish" (No.
136), and "The History of Caelia" (No. 198). Most of the stories,
however, appear intermeshed in the narrative in the form of anecdotes, "portraits," autobiographical sketches or letters, and illustrative episodes—notably the *cumulative episode*, the earliest
example in the essay-serial.[45] In general, three kinds of fiction are
readily apparent in the *Tatler*—namely, the episode (the brief,
imaginary record of a single incident), the tale (two or more
episodes pertaining to the subject under exposition), and the
allegory.

The story types of the *Tatler* also appeared in the *Spectator*,
but the *Tatler* appealed to a slightly different audience taste
through a greater reliance on contemporary news and less emphasis on the "single essay" structure. The salient marks of the
Tatler fiction were to make indelible imprints on its successor.
These outstanding features are noted by Professor Bond:

> The conspicuous marks of *Tatler* fiction were its brevity and
> simplicity, which were essential elements for either a full issue
> of the paper or only part of one. There was no space for com-
> plex plotting with careful motivation and crises and denouement
> or for the development of full-bodied characters, but limited

space was not the only reason for Bickerstaff's simple plots and characterizations. Equally important was the function of the stories, which were used principally to strengthen the editor's purposes of satire and instruction and at times to furnish genial entertainment or sad diversion. The fiction increased as the amount of unmoralized entertainment increased, but with few exceptions the characters were not sharply defined individuals and the narratives seldom had need for very subtle techniques. A broad type of human principle could be illustrated by a broad characterization much more effectively than by a penetrating analysis of a highly individualistic person, and most of the plots simply illuminate a simple theme or moral with a fundamentally simple meaning.[46]

It was this "comparatively artless" fiction of the *Tatler* that helped to make it so readable and agreeable to its generation. It was this successful employment of fresh narrative techniques that later led to the decision by the editors of the *Spectator* to make fiction a more integral part of the purpose and function of the paper. As Bond says, "The *Spectator* was in a sense both a continuation and an imitation of the *Tatler,* retaining, modifying, and omitting characteristics of its predecessor and originating several of its own."[47] Nowhere is this more noticeable than in the *Spectator's* artful employment of "comparatively artless" fictive techniques from the *Tatler.*

Thus it was of this time, and from these antecedents, that the *Spectator* was a product, and all the attempts, successful and unsuccessful, in the motley periodicals from 1690 to 1710 to find "the right combination" that would appeal to the audience of the day helped to prepare the road for its smashing success. The success came not so much because the *Spectator's* authors put their talent into a new art of periodical storytelling but because they put their genius into using the short story superbly as a means to an end: "The mind ought sometimes to be diverted, that it may return to thinking the better."

2

The Character

When I meet with any vicious Character,
that is not generally known, in order to
prevent its doing Mischief, I draw it at
length, and set it up as a Scarecrow. . . .
—Mr. Spectator, *Spectator* No. 205

The character sketch or the Character, as it came to be called in England in the seventeenth century, is one of several types of prose fiction found throughout the *Spectator*. The Character in the *Spectator* is an especially fertile field for the literary critic or historian of prose fiction; the many examples of its use by Addison and Steele attest to its medial position between the old Character and the new "novel." What Addison and Steele did to the form, how they molded it to suit their purposes, and what techniques they accepted, employed, revamped, and anticipated—the answers to all these propositions show that genius was at work, which is not news, but also they indicate what made the *Spectator* succeed. The Character illustrates as much about the adaptability and "looseness" of approach in the *Spectator* as any other classification of its prose fiction.[1]

The Character as a distinct form of literature reached its height in the seventeenth century. By the time the *Spectator* appeared it had been altered to fit the uses of Englishmen; its classic Greek face had been reshaped by Joseph Hall, Sir Thomas Overbury, and John Earle. A few years after the *Spectator*, and with its aid, it was to be virtually absorbed by short periodical fiction, the "novel," and the work of Richardson and Fielding. Totally transcended was the art of Character writing that Theophrastus practiced in Greece around 319 B.C.

Nevertheless, the model that Theophrastus supplied for Character writing was not, at the start of the eighteenth century, without influence.[2] Following Isaac Casaubon's 1592 Latin translation, Theophrastus' *Ethical Characters* had indeed furnished the impetus for the seventeenth-century surge of Character writing. Hall, Overbury, and Earle were all, according to Benjamin Boyce, "Devoted to the memory of Theophrastus,"[3] and whatever changes they introduced never destroyed the Theophrastan center. Theophrastus' method is therefore of utmost importance in any consideration of the Character.[4]

Theophrastus' short accounts in prose of the properties, characteristics, and eccentricities that individualize a type usually follow a set pattern; Richard Aldington describes it as "that balance, temperate good sense, justness and insight, precision of expression, which we mean or ought to mean by the word 'classic.'"[5] Beginning each Character is a brief definition of the primary quality of the person Theophrastus proposes to analyze, and this definition is followed by a variation upon "This man is the sort of person who. . . ." Professor Boyce describes the process very clearly:

> The method in each of these pieces is first to name the moral quality or habit and then very briefly to define it: thus, "Grumbling . . . is an undue complaining of one's lot"; "Garrulity is the delivering of talk that is irrelevant, or long and unconsidered." After the definition comes the main development, the list of actions and speeches that are typical of a victim of the quality under consideration. The picture is built up entirely of details of what the man does or says, usually in apparently random order, as seen or heard by an impersonal observer. Although Theophrastus allows the reader some opportunity to read between the lines, he refrains from explicit statement either of what the character thinks or of what Theophrastus thinks of the character. The language is simple; and almost nothing appears that could be labeled wit.[6]

The Theophrastan Character is presented as a type of moral character primarily "by means of an accumulation of suggestive, characteristic actions and words, and representative of a group of similar individuals."[7] Stylistically, the succession of actions is presented in sentences introduced by the subject pronoun "he" or the noun form "this man." Gwendolen Murphy's definition of the Character embraces these aspects of the form developed by Theophrastus, but it is also elastic enough to apply generally: "The character-sketch is a short, concise, objective account of the properties of a typical person, place, or object which are combined together to make a small whole. . . . In one of the most usual forms the beginning is a definition, frequently conceited, the middle is an accumulation of characteristic traits, . . . the effect being that of a string of adjectives rather than of a reasoned narrative, and the progress is thus not logical but grammatical; the ending tends to be an epigrammatic summary expressed either simply or in a sounding conceit."[8]

Murphy's definition of the Character is sound because it does not fail when applied to those great seventeenth century practitioners: Joseph Hall, Sir Thomas Overbury, John Earle, and Samuel Butler—Addison and Steele's immediate predecessors in the use of the form. Hall probably had the most significant influence on the authors of the *Spectator*, for it was he who made the Character an instrument of didacticism.[9] While openly declaring his allegiance to Theophrastus, he fitted his classical model to the native literary tradition—to be exact, he pitted the legions of Christian virtue against the forces of evil.[10] Hall was interested in the moral and psychological makeup of man, as was Theophrastus, but his interest in the religious condition of men's minds, unlike Overbury and Earle, was a trait that can be observed in the eighteenth-century Character.

Overbury's collection of *Characters* (1614) broadened the scope of Character writing to include places and things and included a greater variety of types. And, rather than showing a tendency toward the ethical introspection of Hall, he allied himself to the comedy of the time. This last trait was used by Addison and Steele, and Mr. Spectator no doubt also profited from what is perhaps Overbury's chief contribution—the "power to make his Characters objectively visible."[11] John Earle, furthermore, in his *Microcosmography* (1628), developed a more-than-superficial ethical analysis of Character. Thomas Fuller's *Holy and Profane States* (1642) freed the character sketch from the Euphuistic tradition, and according to Baldwin it was "henceforth sufficiently elastic in form to be suited to the needs of the periodical essayists of the following century."[12]

The Character was ripe for the uses of Addison, Steele, and the other writers of the *Spectator*. In *Spectator* No. 1 Mr. Spectator says:

> I have been often told by my Friends, that it is Pity so many useful Discoveries which I have made, should be in the Possession of a Silent Man. For this Reason therefore, I shall publish a Sheet-full of Thoughts every Morning, for the Benefit of my Contemporaries; and if I can any way contribute to the Diversion or Improvement of the Country in which I live, I shall leave it . . . with the secret Satisfaction of thinking that I have not Lived in vain. (*Spectator*, I, 5)

And in No. 205 Addison explains his reasons for employing the character sketch:

> When I meet with any vicious Character, that is not generally known, in order to prevent its doing Mischief, I draw it at length, and set it up as a Scarecrow: By which means I do not only make an Example of the Person to whom it belongs, but give Warning to all her Majesty's Subjects that they may not suffer by it. (*Spectator*, II, 302)

Not a few of the "useful Discoveries" Mr. Spectator made regarded the use and form of the Character, and he left it better than he found it. In the *Spectator* the Character was to become an even more elastic form, one that was eventually—and without much more work—to be incorporated into the modern short story.

The Character as written by Addison, Steele, Budgell, and Hughes is, in truth, a "Scarecrow," but its use in the *Spectator* is not wholly functional (as a part of the whole essay), and it is sometimes employed entirely for art's sake. The nature of the subject matter itself demonstrates the authors' concern with the real world—with its flurry of fans being snapped open with military precision in the ladies' chambers, its often ludicruous jockeying for position via the robust eighteenth-century code of courtship, and its den of talk and laughter at the club and tavern—rather than with rarefied philosophical, abstract, and analytical theories of conduct and thought. Social types, such as "The Demurrer" (No. 89), "The Jilt" (No. 187), "The Talkative" (No. 247), and "The Pleasant Fellow" (No. 462), predominate, although a moral quality is often suggested in a type, too, as in "The Virtuous Woman" (No. 302), "The Envious Man" (No. 19), and "The Charitable Man" (No. 177). The Characters, socially oriented as they are, certainly bring "Philosophy out of Closets and Libraries, Schools and Colleges, to dwell in Clubs and Assemblies, at Tea-Tables, and in Coffee-Houses" (*Spectator*, I, 44) and provide a variegated portrait of the domestic, club, romantic, political, educational, fashion, and daily routine life of London and the countryside. While the portrait or Character is not judged on the scale of didacticism, one is never quite unaware of the frame of right conduct that surrounds it or the light of reason that shines over it.

Part of the appeal of the Character is due to the tendency of Addison and Steele to move from the general to the particular in their choice of subject matter for characterization. Such topics as John Earle's "A Child," "A Young Man," and "A Good Old Man;" Joseph Hall's "Wise Man," "Honest Man," and "Faithful Man;" and Sir Thomas Overbury's "The Proud Man" were naturally not excluded, but there is a clear development toward what Benjamin Boyce terms "a strong sense of the local fact, perhaps at the expense of universality."[13] For example, Steele on one occasion chose to write a Character of "The Affectedly Unconcerned

and the Affectedly Busy" (No. 284) when the tradition behind
the form might logically have suggested simply "The Busy Man."
Sometimes the precision of the authors can be observed in the
presentation of slightly variant aspects of people who are actually
of the same general type: two examples are "The Inquisitive (No.
228) and "The Unduly Curious" (No. 439), "The Male Jilt" (No.
288) and "The Henpecked Husband" (No. 176). This stricter par-
ticularization in a number of the Characters is of course most
readily noticed in the label names often given to the characters or
to the narrators of the Characters; generally the use of "classical'"
names (Arsene, Cresus, etc.) is avoided for the more familiarly
English ones of Charles Yellow, Isaac Hedgeditch, and Nathaniel
Henroost.

Clearly, then, social-moral rather than professional and philosophical types are the usual subject matter for the Characters, and
the types are Englished at every opportunity. But how can the
Characters be classified in order to analyze most tellingly what
Addison and Steele either contributed or helped to popularize in
the area of short narrative fiction? A classification according to
author immediately suggests itself as perhaps the most clear-cut—
and it is interesting that Steele wrote twice as many of the forty-
odd Characters as Addison—but this classification hinders a concentration on their methods of handling the form that are not
noticeably distinctive.[14] A classification according to whether a
Character concerns a man, a woman, or both is simply too oriented toward what is written rather than how or with what effect;
it makes little difference, for example, to know the simple fact
that the ratio is 3–1–1. Actually, the most useful and convenient
method of classifying the character sketches is by dividing them
into typical and individual types, which Melvin R. Watson in
Magazine Serials and the Essay Tradition 1746–1820[15] defines as
"those in which the type predominates and those in which individual traits predominate."

This kind of grouping allows greater freedom to investigate
style and techniques employed to achieve readability, interest,

and variety. The "typical" Characters fall into two categories: (1) the formal, brief, objective Character that is closely related to the Theophrastan and seventeenth-century form of the type, and (2) the informal, looser-organized, subjective Character that bears the influence of La Bruyère.[16] The "individual" group contains those Characters that not only represent a type but also are so portrayed that they seem almost to be real people—or, more significantly, believable characters involved in a good measure of quasi-fictional actions and conflicts. The methods Addison, Steele, Budgell, and Hughes employed in these three classes of Characters in the *Spectator* reveal a continuing loosening of the form to fit narrative needs. Using three general approaches—whether by the biographical account, directly by description, or indirectly through action—the authors come close, in a number of cases, to achieving the limited action, some conflict, unity of mood, and character interplay necessary for the short story proper. It is not, however, the purpose here to prove that a few of the *Spectator*'s Characters are long-lost short stories; rather, this classification of the Characters in the *Spectator* should aid in an appreciation of Mr. Spectator's approach and techniques in the use of the form and indicate a greater use of fictional techniques than has been pointed out previously.

Those Characters in the *Spectator* that reflect most distinctly the formal and objective Theophrastan Character, which was initiated in England by Joseph Hall, are comparatively few. They are creations with little imagination; touch after touch is simply added one after the other, each one of which indicates the same characteristic from different points of view. Wit and the verisimilitude of the portrayal carry the burden of catching the interest of the reader, who normally can detect no logical arrangement of ideas in the sketch. Characters in this group remain types, and nothing more. Into this category belong Steele's "The Woman's Man" (No. 156), "The Mercurial Friend" (No. 194), "The Inconsistent and Extravagant" (No. 222), "The Devotée" (No. 354), "The Pleasant Fellow" (No. 462), and "The Punster" (No. 504);

and Addison's "The Jealous Husband" (No. 170), "The Charitable Man" (No. 177), "The Salamander" (No. 198), "The Ambitious Man" (No. 255), and "The Unduly Curious" (No. 439).

Five of these Characters (Nos. 156, 170, 198, 255, and 504) contain few elements of prose narrative and represent a method of handling the material that follows the formal pattern of Theophrastus and his seventeenth-century followers Hall and Overbury. There occurs the definition of the quality at the very beginning, followed by a straightforward accumulation of actions to illustrate the trait objectively and scientifically before a formal conclusion. Addison uses this classic approach in "The Jealous Husband" (No. 170), a very serious piece; *"Jealousy,"* Mr. Spectator begins, *"is that Pain which a Man feels from the Apprehension that he is not equally beloved by the Person whom he entirely loves"* (*Spectator,* II, 168).[17] This set beginning is varied slightly in Nos. 156 and 198—the focus is placed on the concrete, the person with the quality: Steele opens his Character by writing that "The Woman's Man is a Person in his Air and Behaviour quite different from the rest of our Species: His Garb is more loose and negligent, his Manner more soft and indolent; that is to say, in both these Cases there is an apparent Endeavour to appear unconcerned and careless" (*Spectator,* II, 111); and Addison in No. 198, loosening the formula's rigid and serious tone even more, immediately begins in a similar way—"Now a Salamander is a kind of Heroine in Chastity, that treads upon Fire, and lives in the Midst of Flames without being hurt" (*Spectator,* II, 275–76).

Addison goes on in No. 198 to give a strictly serious analysis of the ambitious man, and—as in the other four Characters mentioned above—the putative author, Mr. Spectator, is left completely in the background as the emphasis is placed on the abstract quality. This practice results in a general depiction that leaves no room for character development, as this example from "The Salamander" (No. 198) illustrates: "She admits a Male Visitant to her Bed-side, plays with him a whole Afternoon at Pickette, walks with him two or three Hours by Moon-light; and is extreamly

Scandalized at the unreasonableness of an Husband, or the severity of a Parent, that would debar the Sex from such innocent
Liberties" (*Spectator*, II, 276). This kind of straightforward build-
up of actions is somewhat more specific and localized in "The
Punster" (No. 504), which gives a few examples of puns, but this
Character, like the others, is typical in its impersonality and universality and adherence to a formal pattern. The formal pattern
includes the rhetorical finale, reminiscent of Overbury's, which
was often introduced by "lastly" or "to conclude" and was en-
forced by an epigram.[18] Addison ends "The Jealous Husband"
with a "as we have seen all along," and the conclusion to "The
Salamander" is equally formal and epigrammatic: "In short, the
Salamander lives in an invincible State of Simplicity and Innocence: Her Constitution is *preserv'd* in a kind of natural Frost;
She wonders what People mean by Temptations; and defies Mankind to do their worst" (*Spectator*, II, 172; II, 276).

Some effort is made, even in these most formal "typical" Characters, to add an element of individuality. This is achieved simply
by assigning a name to the character that is otherwise presented
as a type and in the traditional way. In "The Pleasant Fellow"
(No. 462) Steele begins his brief sketch by stating, "*Dacinthus* is
neither in point of Honour, Civility, good Breeding, or good Nature unexceptionable, and yet all is answer'd, *For he is a very
pleasant Fellow*" (*Spectator*, IV, 131). Just how much the addition of such a classical name heightened the audience's interest
in the object as an individual is, naturally, a matter of conjecture,
but it was a step toward individuality. On one occasion, however,
in Addison's "The Unduly Curious" (No. 439), the reportorial approach was used, that is, Mr. Spectator's Character must be that
of an individual, even though presented formally, since the man
did actually exist. "I shall conclude this Essay," writes Mr. Spectator, "with Part of a Character which is finely drawn by the Earl
of *Clarendon*, in the first Book of his History, and which gives us
the lively Picture of a great Man teizing himself with an absurd
Curiosity" (*Spectator*, IV, 45). This insistence on the truth of the

Character—and the assigning of a name, however bookish—is perhaps still more striking in Addison's "The Charitable Man" (No.
177). Writing of charity as a moral virtue, Mr. Spectator stops
short and explains that "This may possibly be explained better
by an Example than by a Rule" (*Spectator*, II, 198). The Character of the "Charitable Man" that follows illustrates beautifully
how Addison gives only the semblance of writing about a real
person, without employing any truly fictional techniques. "Eugenius is a Man of an Universal Good-nature," the typical beginning reads, and then Mr. Spectator sets forth traits and actions
in the old Theophrastan manner: "Eugenius has,'" "he makes,"
"Eugenius prescribes," "he goes," "he is," etc. The narrator's as-
surance that "I have known him"—in addition to the name—also
helps to make the account appear as truth, a report. Here is the
narrator in the fictional tradition of the reporter of events, a role
later developed more extensively in *Moll Flanders*.

In three of the formal "typical" Characters, Addison and Steele
used the letter-from-a-correspondent device, which they often
used more imaginatively, as will be noted in the following discussion of the informal "typical" Characters and the "individual"
Characters. No. 222, "The Inconsistent and Extravagent" (Steele),
opens with a letter from a correspondent, who remains nameless,
as does the subject, but the device effectively varies the point of
view and again serves to emphasize the "truth" of the account.
Steele's brief sketch of "The Mercurial Friend" (No. 194) likewise
employs an unsigned letter—this time with no additional remarks
by Mr. Spectator—to present the Character, which contains few
specific details but several general actions and descriptions of the
friend's changes of mood. In Steele' s"The Devotée" (No. 354),
however, the correspondent signs his name, "Hotspur," though the
proffered Character is no more individualized or imaginative than
the other Theophrastan-like ones of the group now under discussion.

A *Devotée* is one of those who disparage Religion by their in-

discreet and unseasonable Introduction of the mention of Virtue
on all Occasions: She professes she is what no Body ought to
doubt she is, and betrays the Labour she is put to, to be what
she ought to be with Chearfullness and Alacrity. . . . She is
never her self but at Church; there she displays her Vertue, and
is so fervent in her Devotions, that I have frequently seen her
Pray her self out of Breath. (*Spectator,* III, 320)

Thus Mr. Spectator blends wit and verisimilitude in the Theo-
phrastan-Hall-Overbury manner in three formal "typical" Characters. The device of the letter, though a promising effect, does not
achieve its full potential.

In the second category the "typical" Characters are more loose-
ly organized, rather more subjective in tone, and on the whole less
formally structured. They are more like human beings because the
complexity of man is made explicitly evident, but they remain
types.[19] For purposes of discussion, this category also may be
divided into three parts: (1) "typical" Characters that are presented by Mr. Spectator only, that imaginatively reveal the Character directly through description, indirectly through action, or
through a brief biographical survey; (2) "typical" Characters in-
volving letters from correspondents; and (3) "typical" Characters
that present various sides of personality through the presence of
more than one character—individual—in the sketch. The first division includes "The Envious Man" (No. 19), "The Pict" (No.
41), "The Idol" (73), "The Courtier" (No. 193), "The Agreeable
Man" (No. 280), "The Virtuous Woman" (No. 302), "The Benevolent Man" (No. 467), "The Biter" (No. 504), and "The Absent-
minded Man," from La Bruyère (No. 77).

Steele's "The Envious Man" (No. 19), a very orderly account
that leaves no feeling of haphazard recollections (a trait common
with the Theophrastan technique), contains some excellent indi-
cations of how Steele elasticized the Character in the direction of
realism and believability and indeed realistic short fiction. The
beginning sentence offers an interesting contrast to Theophrastan
pithiness:

Observing one Person behold another, who was an utter Stranger
to him, with a Cast of his Eye, which, methought, expressed an
Emotion of Heart very different from what could be raised by
an Object so agreeable as the Gentleman he looked at, I began
to consider, not without some secret Sorrow, the Condition of
an Envious Man. (*Spectator,* I, 82–83)

Theophrastus, and normally his seventeenth-century followers
Hall and Overbury, would have begun, most likely, with a statement such as "Envy causes man much pain, few reliefs, and no
happiness." Stylistically, the beginning in no way reflects the brevity in clauses or sentences, a lack of symmetry in the parts of a
sentence, the obscurity, and the toughness that characterized the
seventeenth-century Character.[20] Steele still introduces the quality
to be discussed in the opening sentence, but there is a difference.
It must be remembered, of course, that he does have a fictional
narrator about whom the reader has already learned a great deal;
the "I" telling the account therefore immediately prepares the
reader for a more personal revelation than the third-person Characters earlier had afforded.

The narrator, Mr. Spectator, is subjective and projects himself
into the situation; he views the situation, we are told, "not without some secret Sorrow." Yet it is Steele's embryonic insistence on
a straightforward setting of the scene, and the situation at hand,
that most anticipates the tried techniques of short prose fiction.
There is not a full picture or image of the actual specific location,
but the realistic touch of noticing one man observing another
"with a Cast of his Eye" that in turn "expressed an Emotion of
Heart" focuses immediate attention on a single incident. In the
opening sentence Steele achieves an immediacy that the old Characters failed to accomplish so quickly; he establishes a personal
raison d'être for his reflections, to which the subsequent traits
may be linked.

The organization of "The Envious Man" is tight; Steele limits
the discussion of the type to three specific areas—his pains, his
reliefs, his happiness—and a paragraph is devoted to each. Fur-

thermore, Mr. Spectator does not point out actions one after the
other with no apparent order. In the paragraph on "Pains," for
example, he carefully gives the Character some individuality
while at the same time maintaining its universal application as
a type. Noticeably, he avoids the anaphoristic "He was . . . He is
. . . He does" pattern by employing a useful device: the addition
of another character, who is given a local habitation and name
("Will Prosper"). The device allows Steele to present the "quality" of the type—envy—through an (admittedly slight) interaction
of people. The image is at least not static: Will Prosper "*points* to
such an handsom Young Fellow, and *whispers* that he is secretly
married to a Great Fortune: When they doubt, he adds Circumstances to prove it; and never fails to aggravate their Distress, by
assuring 'em that to his knowledge he has an Uncle [who] will
leave him some Thousands" (*Spectator*, I, 83. Italics mine).

In the paragraph on "Reliefs" of the envious man, another rudimentary fictional technique is evident. Steele, through Mr. Spectator, portrays a group of envious men sitting around a table
presenting their ideas about a poet who has written an excellent
poem. To accomplish the didactic purpose "a certain honest Fellow" interrupts and makes a subjective comment on their actions.
"An honest Fellow," Mr. Spectator says, "who sate among a Clus-
ter of them in debate on this Subject, cryed out, *Gentlemen, if you
are sure none of you your selves had an hand in it, you are but
where you were, whoever writ it*" (*Spectator*, I, 84). This use of
the actual spoken words of a man to add subjectivity, as well as
an element of realism and immediacy, is a significant departure from
the normal practice and improves the narrative trend of the account.

At the conclusion of "The Envious Man" Steele brings the
reader back to a consideration of the first-person narrator and to a
reflection upon the opening scene: "In the mean while, if any one
says the *Spectator* has Wit, it may be some Relief to them, to think
that he does not show it in Company. And if any one praises his
Morality, they may comfort themselves by considering that his

Face is none of the longest" (*Spectator*, I, 85). This Character
has a unity, then, that is both apparent and real; it also has subjectivity and the portrayal, in a comparatively realistic manner, of
"real" people who help to reveal the typical, less realistic type—
The Envious Man. Most interestingly, the situation moves the narrator, Mr. Spectator. "The Envious Man" is not merely a static
exercise in Theophrastan form. Steele extends the Character both
in the direction of the well-organized essay and unified, economic,
realistic, and imaginative short fiction with limited action, characters, and theme.

The method of handling the material in Addison's "The Idol"
(No. 73), as in "The Envious Man," involves Mr. Spectator, the
first-person fictional narrator. The opening portion of the Character contains general traits and actions of the type, but a clear
attempt is made to look at a specific person, Clarinda, as one of
the greatest idols. The details presented in describing the setting
and telling what is happening add specificity to the typicality:

> She is Worshipped once a Week by Candle-light in the midst
> of a large Congregation generally called an Assembly. Some of
> the gayest Youths in the Nation endeavour to plant themselves
> in her Eye, while she sits in form with multitudes of Tapers
> burning about her. (*Spectator*, I, 314)[21]

The details also serve a metaphorical function—"Tapers" parallels
"gayest youths." Even though there are some detailed descriptions, a named character, and a description of her actions, there is
not, in any sense, any real depiction of the Character as a believable individual. Her movements are related cursorily:

> To encourage the Zeal of her Idolaters, she bestows a Mark of
> her Favour upon every one of them before they go out of her
> Presence. She asks a Question of one, tells a Story to another,
> glances an Ogle upon a third, takes a Pinch of Snuff from a
> fourth. . . . (*Spectator*, I, 314)

The slight divergence from the formal pattern through use of details and a name does not achieve believable individuality in this

Character; even so, it is obvious that Addison was working to-ward that end.

In No. 41 Steele had depicted a Character quite similar to "The Idol," one that he called "The Pict." They afford interesting comparisons because they show how refined the art of distinction in types had become by this time. The method of introducing the subject and handling the material is essentially the same as in "The Idol" (Mr. Spectator narrates), but in this instance a letter—though not a part of the Character itself—is used as a catalyst. The letter from a correspondent broaches the topic through its discussion of the writer's wife, one of those women whose every attribute is a work of art—painted on. The technique of presenting the Character at first offers no surprises: "The *Picts*, tho' never so Beautiful, have dead, uninformed Countenances" (*Spectator*, I, 174). Still in a general survey, Mr. Spectator broadens his perspective, and with gentle, humorous satire he writes that

> A *Pict*, tho' she takes all that Pains to invite the Approach of Lovers, is obliged to keep them a certain Distance; a Sigh in a Languishing Lover, if fetched too near her, would dissolve a Feature; and a Kiss snatched by a Forward one, might transfer the Complexion of the Mistress to the Admirer. (*Spectator*, I, 174–75)

At this point Steele inserts a narrative episode to highlight the qualities of "The Pict" more vividly. Mr. Spectator relates Will Honeycomb's adventure with a Pict, in which he falls in love, is spurned, goes to see her at her apartment, sees her choosing her face for the day, and leaves, shaken. Here again the type is presented, but it is presented in conjunction with a flesh-and-blood character, Will Honeycomb. It is a delightfully humorous and credible story. A scene is depicted. Interaction between two forces occurs. When she sees him observing her the Pict "stood before him in the utmost Confusion, with the prettiest Smirk imaginable on the finish'd side of her Face, pale as Ashes on the other" (*Spectator*, I, 175). In the episode there is a dramatic tension and enough story element to involve the reader. The ending is especially appealing: "HONEYCOMB seized all her Gally-Pots and Washes, and carried off his Handkerchief full of Brushes, Scraps of *Spanish* Wool, and Phials of Unguents. The Lady went into the Country, the Lover was cured" (*Spectator,* I, 175-76). The character development remains weak, but here Steele has adapted the form of the Character to the use of short narrative prose. There is—however sketchy—character interaction, a specific setting, a conscious and unified thematic purpose, and a plot to catch a lover unawares.

Will Honeycomb also figures in Budgell's account of "The Absend-minded Man" (No. 77), which follows closely the English translation of it in La Bruyère's *Characters* (Third Edition, London, 1702).[22] Before the Character of Menalcas begins, Budgell relates an anecdote, also from La Bruyère, which is reminiscent of the scene in which Honeycomb was involved in "The Pict." It is the famous episode of Will's walking with Mr. Spectator, looking at his watch, throwing it in the river, and pocketing a pebble. Characteristically the adaptation is put in an English setting—"A little before our Club-time last Night we were walking together in *Somerset* Garden . . ." (*Spectator,* I, 329)—before Mr. Spectator, adopting a personal, rather confidential tone, defines what he means by an absent-minded man by addressing the reader directly: "My Reader does, I hope, perceive, that I distinguish a Man who is *Absent,* because he thinks of something else, from one who is *Absent,* because he thinks of nothing at all: The latter is too Innocent a Creature to be taken notice of: but the Distractions of the former may, I believe, be generally accounted for . . ." (*Spectator,* I, 330). As in "The Pict" Mr. Spectator at this point introduces a personal experience; Will Honeycomb at the coffeehouse sees Mr. Spectator, talks about him, and then later meets him on the street and chats as if he had not seen him earlier. This realistic touch, this little scene, complete with dialogue, provides a narrative link with the beginning and achieves a certain unity, and at the same time it prepares the way for the presentation of the Character of Menalcas from La Bruyère.

Some of these same techniques are present in Steele's "The Biter" (No. 504), which also presents a "typical" Character in a manner that transcends the formal methods of the Theophrastan school. The sketch begins in a predictable manner: "In a Word, a Biter is one who thinks you a Fool, because you do not think him a Knave" (*Spectator*, IV, 289). But Mr. Spectator again attempts to make the Character seem more than a type by employing narrative techniques that tend to suggest the portrait of this kind of person at work rather than the theoretical tractlike depiction of a universal quality of behavior. For example, according to Mr. Spectator:

> There came up a shrewd young Fellow to a plain young Man, his Countryman, and taking him aside with a grave concern'd Countenance, goes on at this rate: I see you here, and have you heard nothing out of *Yorkshire*—You look so surpriz'd you could not have heard of it—and yet the Particulars are such, that it cannot be false: I am sorry I am got into it so far, that I now must tell you; but I know not but it may be for your Service to know—On *Tuesday* last, just after Dinner— you know his Manner is to smoke, opening his Box, your Father fell down dead in an Apoplexy. The Youth shew'd the filial Sorrow which he ought —Upon which the witty Man cry'd, *Bite, there was nothing in all this*— (*Spectator*, IV, 289–90)

The record of the actual spoken words, presented in such a way as to convey the conversational tone and the sting of the wit, is a technique that amplifies the generalities of the type and becomes a short narrative episode.

Also included in the first group of the second category of Characters are "The Courtier" (No. 193), "The Virtuous Woman" (No. 302), "The Agreeable Man" (No. 280), and "The Benevolent Man" (No. 467). In all four a continued effort is made to infuse some realistic details and to employ the subjective approach of the narrator, Mr. Spectator. The method of handling the material is the same as in the other Characters of this group discussed above. Whether revealed directly by description, as in the Characters "The Benevolent Man" (named Manilius) and "The Agreeable Man" (named Polycarpus), or indirectly through actions, Mr. Spectator's aim is to convince the reader insofar as possible that the person is real or that the actions are true. In Hughes's "The Virtuous Woman" (No. 302) it is made clear that "the Character of *Emilia* is not an imaginary but a real one" (*Spectator,* III, 79). In Steele's "The Courtier" (No. 193) the approach or technique is more like that of "The Biter"—conversation is recorded between the Great Man and those he comforts in his comings and goings. The details of the moment, the offhand comments of Mr. Spectator, and the loosened structure are evidences of a technique of presentation and a method of handling the material that make for good narrative prose. To be sure, these fictional techniques had not produced much beyond a type; for, as Mr. Spectator notes in "The Courtier" (No. 193), "the chief Point is to keep in Generals; and if there be any thing offered that's Particular, to be in haste" (*Spectator,* II, 259). In his haste, fortunately, Mr. Spectator left significant contributions to the art of short prose narrative.

In a number of the less formal "typical" Characters the point of view is not that of Mr. Spectator since the character types either describe themselves or are described by another party. The fictional point of view remains, and the letter device in this category of Characters is normally used with more freedom than in the first category of formal "typical" Characters. The technique of the correspondent and handling the material primarily through the appearance of a letter may be observed in Steele's "The Castle-builder" (No. 167), Addison's "The Valetudinarian" (No. 25), Steele's "The Free-thinker" (No. 234), Steele's "The Tyrannical Husband" (No. 236), Steele's "The Male Jilt, or The Fribbler" (No. 288), Addison's "The Cott-quean" (No. 482), and Steele's "The Club-tyrant" (No. 508). The subject matter, as is evident from the titles, continues to be basically social and moral rather than philosophical and professional in nature.

In two of these Characters, Nos. 167 and 25, the correspondents describe themselves in a letter to the editor. The first-person account that results thus has a kind of inherent reality, immediacy, and subjectivity that the old Characters lacked. Noteworthy also is the fact that Mr. Spectator's purpose is not to teach but to amuse with these Characters: "There is little pursued in the Errors . . . of these Worthies, but mere present Amusement . . ." (*Spectator,* II, 158). Although Mr. Spectator recognized that entertaining the reader called for the variation of an old form, the letter from the Castle-builder, Vitruvius, does not in practice offer tangible evidence that the man is more than a representative of a type. He is short, he is a Protestant, but typical he remains: "A Castle-Builder is even just what he pleases, and as such I have grasped imaginary Scepters, and delivered uncontroulable Edicts from a Throne to which conquer'd Nations yielded Obeysance" (*Spectator,* II, 159).

Typical, too, is the letter Character from "The Valetudinarian," who does not sign his name; but there is a feeling of individuality in his letter whether analysis can prove it or not. Instead of setting forth numerous actions of a type, the letter writer makes his account realistic through details. In relating the incident of his staying in the Mathematical Chair, a sort of scales, in order to keep his weight at two hundred pounds, the reader is saturated with specific details until he *knows* he is confronted with a person, not a type, but of course it is an illusion:

> "In my greatest Excesses I do not transgress more than the other half Pound; which, for my Healths sake, I do the first *Monday* in every Month. As soon as I find my self duly poised after Dinner, I walk till I have perspired five Ounces and four Scruples; and when I discover, by my Chair, that I am so far reduced, I fall to my Books, and Study away three Ounces more." (*Spectator,* I, 106)[23]

The conflict, like the writer, has a universal application, for it reveals the foolishness of the struggle within his own being.

The remaining five "typical" Characters that employ the letter device (Nos. 234, 288, 482, 508, 236) are from individuals who describe a person close to them. Perhaps the most interesting of these Characters is Steele's "The Free-thinker" (No. 234), which creates a curiosity in the character as an individual—before noting his dominant quality—in prose that has a smooth narrative texture:

> "There arrived in this Neighbourhood two Days ago one of your gay Gentlemen of the Town, who being attended at his Entry with a Servant of his own, besides a Countryman he had taken up for a Guide, excited the Curiosity of the Village to learn whence and what he might be." (*Spectator*, II, 411)[24]

Also a rather clever device is Steele's use of the Countryman, another observer, to provide a subjective definition of "free-thinker":

> "What Religion that might be, he could not tell, and for his own part, if they had not told him the Man was a Free-thinker, he should have guessed, by his way of talking, he was little better than a Heathen; excepting only that he had been a good Gentleman to him, and made him drunk twice in one Day, over and above what they had bargain'd for." (*Spectator*, II, 412)

The comment is subjective, but, more than that, it illustrates the effective use by Steele of an ignorant character to produce humor and irony. The counrtyman one smiles at represents the common view. The same method and similar techniques are evident in Steele's "The Male Jilt" (No. 288), where Melainia offers a prejudiced view, and "The Club-tyrant" (No. 508), where the writer righteously proclaims, "I shall give an Account of the King of the Company I am fallen into, whom for his particular Tyranny I shall call *Dionysius;* as also of the Seeds that sprung up to this odd Sort of Empire" (*Spectator*, IV, 302). Addison's "The Cott-quean" (No. 482), a letter from a female reader, likewise presents a type, although the possibilities of uniqueness are evident in her opening remarks: "I have the Misfortune to be joined for Life with one of this Character, who in reality is more a Woman than I am" (*Spectator,* IV, 210). It is Steele's "The Tyrannical Husband" (No. 236) that employs a device not yet mentioned: the rhetorical question. The unnamed writer submits question after question—all of which help to define the type—and in this manner draws the reader, perhaps unconsciously, into the account and demands a response (See *Spectator,* II, 417).

Four Characters of this second category, the informal "typical" Characters, employ a method of handling the subject that deserves attention. In these Mr. Spectator, or a letter writer, presents not one but two or three characters to represent the general type, and usually the characters are named. In Steele's "The Affectedly Unconcerned and the Affectedly Busy" (No. 284), the qualities are distinguished via letters from first one type and then the other. After discussing the general characteristics, Mr. Spectator tries to breathe life into the type by producing letters from Stephen Courtier and Bridget Eitherdown (*Spectator,* III, 7-8). In Addison's "The Demurrer'" (No. 89) the quality is introduced in the first sentence, but, instead of following the Theophrastan pattern of listing separate actions of one demurrer, he presents several:

> I find by another Letter from one who calls himself *Thirsis,* that his Mistress has been Demurring above these seven Years. But among all my Plaintiffs of this nature, I most pity the unfortunate *Philander,* a Man of a constant Passion and plentiful Fortune, who sets forth that the timorous and irresolute *Sylvia* has demurred till she is past Child-bearing. *Strephon* appears by his Letter to be a very Cholerick Lover. . . . (*Spectator,* I, 377)

This is, of course, only the appearance of individualism, but it serves almost to trick the reader into seeing people rather than lifeless types. Mr. Spectator, again, is not the old omniscient third-person narrator. What he relates has been told to him, often, he insists, "with great Passion" (*Spectator,* I, 377). In this case, Sam

Hopewell, the writer of the letter, turns out to be a perfectly believable victim of the demurring woman even as he serves to plant the moral lesson: "We often lament that we did not marry sooner, but she has no Body to blame for it but her self. You know very well that she would never think of me whilst she had a Tooth in her Head" (*Spectator*, I, 378).

Addison's "The Talkative" (No. 247) describes four classes of the type, and in doing so Addison employs four varying techniques. The first class, the stirrers of passion, is a quite brief section that relies on humor and suggestion to carry the point. In describing the stirring of passion, there is hardly need to say more than that it is "a part of Rhetorick in which *Socrates* his Wife had perhaps made a greater Proficiency" than Socrates (*Spectator*, II, 459). The censorious, the second division of the talkative type, are suggested through the use of the rhetorical question, which relates the general description:

> The Imagination and Elocution of this Sett of Rhetoricians is wonderful. With what a fluency of Invention, and Copiousness of Expression, will they enlarge upon every little slip in the behavior of another? With how many different Circumstances, and with what variety of Phrases, will they tell over the same Story? (*Spectator*, II, 459)

At this point the story of an old lady "I have known" is told, the Character being portrayed indirectly through action. Choosing an opposing technique Addison depicts the gossips, the third class, directly through the description of Mrs. Fiddle Faddle. The coquette then is presented by enumerating several of the actions of this class around the town, and one is not conscious of Mr. Spectator's fictional narration in the rather formal method: "The Coquet is in particular a great Mistress of that part of Oratory which is called Action, and indeed seems to speak for no other Purpose, but as it gives her an Opportunity of stirring a Limb, or varying a Feature, of glancing her Eyes, or playing with her Fan" (*Spectator*, II, 459).

Steele's "The Jilt" (No. 187) illustrates much of the same method of approach as Addison uses in "The Talkative." Again the letter device is used as three sides of the same type are portrayed. Charles Yellow, the correspondent, moves from a serious to lighthearted to serious tone in the discussion of Corinna, Kitty, and Hyaena—the three principal representatives of classes of jilts. Corinna, who tormented men until all found her out, is described objectively and with pity; but Kitty, Yellow's old mistress, receives humorous treatment of her "Wild, Thoughtless and Irregular" ways (*Spectator,* II, 236). Yellow indicates that this experience taught him a lesson—until he met Hyaena, the third example of a jilt, one who does not mind the inconstancy of her lovers, "provided she can boast she once had their Addresses" (*Spectator,* II, 237). In this Character, and in Nos. 89, 284, and 247 above, the loosening of form and the imaginative variation of the old Theophrastan method through various techniques of style, structure, and character expansion are striking.

The last category of Characters in the *Spectator* is the one in which Addison and Steele most successfully transform the purely typical into the decidedly individual. There is a noticeable tendency to show characters in action and through conflict of interests rather than to describe indirectly the traits of a type. Using the same method of handling (such as a letter from a correspondent), the result is often the kernel of a short story. Steele's "The Henpecked Husband" (No. 176) becomes a little autobiographical short story in which Mr. Spectator does not intrude at all: "There are in the following Letter Matters which I, a Batchelor, cannot be supposed to be acquainted with; therefore [I] shall not pretend to explain upon it till further Consideration, but leave the Author of the Epistle to express his Condition his own Way" (*Spectator,* II, 193–94). This insistence on truth of course was expected in the fiction of the time, but the credibility of the story is also seen in the way the narrator, Nathaniel Henroost, moves the emphasis from the general quality of male passivity to a specific picture of a henpecked man in London to a particular view of one man—Henroost himself—as a living example of the type. There is an unmistakable outline of a continued action between characters, individuals who talk to each other:

> "She will sometimes look at me with an assumed Grandeur, and pretend to resent that I have not had Respect enough for her Opinion in such an Instance in Company. I cannot but smile at the pretty Anger she is in, and then she pretends she is used like a Child. . . . She is eternally forming an Argument of Debate; to which I very indolently answer, Thou art mighty pretty. To this she answers, All the World but you think I have as much Sense as your self. I repeat to her, Indeed you are Pretty. Upon this there is no Patience; she will throw down any thing about her, stamp, and pull off her Head-Cloaths. Fie, my Dear, say I; how can a Woman of your Sense fall into such an intemperate Rage? This is an Argument which never fails. Indeed, my Dear, says she, you make me mad sometimes, so you do, with the silly Way you have of treating me like a pretty Idiot." (*Spectator*, II, 195)

This use of dialogue goes a long way toward achieving individuality, but the reality is capped by the neatness of the closing statement, where one can imagine Henroost's hurriedly prepared final words, "I have ten thousand thousand things more to say, but my Wife sees me writing, and will, according to Custom, be consulted if I do not seal this immediately" (*Spectator*, II, 196). A type is shown, but an individual is speaking.

The same kind of "individual" Character is revealed in the narrative episode related by Mr. Spectator in Steele's "The Inquisitive" (No. 228). Here Mr. Spectator tells of sitting in a public room and noting the clash between a talker and an inquisitive man:

> The Man of ready Utterance sat down by him; and rubbing his Head, leaning on his Arm, and making an uneasy Countenance, he began; "There is no Manner of News to Day. I cannot tell what is the Matter with me, but I slept very ill last Night; whether I caught Cold or no I know not, but I fancy I do not

wear Shooes thick enough for the Weather, and I have coughed all the Week: It must be so. . . ." (*Spectator,* II, 386)

The long-winded fellow thus reveals his own Character, and Mr. Spectator relates how this "talk about nothing" delights the Inquisitive Man, who repeats all this *verbatim* to another person when the Talker leaves. The sketch does indeed prove that the inquisitive man is a funnel of conversation, but Steele's technique of presentation also suggests an individual in contact with real people drinking in a tavern.[25]

The way Steele moves from the universally general to the particularly individual—from essay to story—is superbly ilustrated in his "The Angry Man" (No. 438). In the first part the narrator, Mr. Spectator, gives the general nature of the passionate man. Then indirectly through actions he describes a typical example, Syncropius, who is made somewhat more realistic through the recording of his spoken words in various situations. Steele ends this section in a manner reminiscent of Joseph Hall: "In a Word, to eat with, or visit *Syncropius,* is no other than going to see him exercise his Family, exercise their Patience, and his own Anger" (*Spectator,* IV, 40). At this point Mr. Spectator draws a portrait of the snarler, a particular sort of angry man. The narrative qualities exhibited are abundant:

> There came into the Shop a very learned Man with an erect Solemn Air, and tho' a Person of great Parts otherwise, slow in understanding any thing which makes against himself. The Composure of the faulty Man, and the whimsical perplexity of him that was justly angry, is perfectly New: After turning over many Volumes, said the Seller to the Buyer, *Sir, you know I have long asked you to send me back the first Volume of French Sermons I formerly lent you;* Sir, said the Chapman, I have often looked for it but cannot find it; It is certainly lost, and I know not to whom I lent it, it is so many Years ago; *then Sir, here is the other Volume, I'll send you home that, and please to pay for both.* My Friend, reply'd he, can'st thou be so Senseless as not to know that one Volume is as imperfect in my Library as your

Shop. *Yes, Sir, but it is you have lost the first Volume, and to
be short I will be Paid.* Sir, answer'd the Chapman, you are a
Young Man, your Book is lost, and learn by this little Loss to
bear much greater Adversities, which you must expect to meet
with. *Yes, Sir, I'll bear when I must, but I have not lost now,
for I say you have it and shall Pay me.* Friend you grow Warm,
I tell you the Book is lost, and I foresee in the Course even of a
prosperous Life, that you will meet Afflictions to make you Mad,
if you cannot bear this Trifle. *Sir, there is in this Case no need
of bearing, for you have the Book. . . .* (*Spectator*, IV, 41–42)

This episode, with its two characters in conflict, with its unified
thematic emphasis, with its specific setting, with its limited action,
imaginatively reveals the exasperation of one and the sly patience
of another individual.

Three other Steele sketches, "The Match-maker" (No. 437),
"The Model Daughter" (No. 449), and "The Frugal, Retired
Man" (No. 264), approach the realm of the "individual" Character. Realistic details and several characters in *motion* make "The
Match-maker" a delightful narrative story. Beginning from "The
other Day pass'd by me in her Chariot a Lady, with that pale
and wan Complexion," Mr. Spectator places the emphasis on real
people, who apparently incidentally represent types. Minute details of movement and gesture, conversation, and exact setting
description transform Sempronia and her dealings with Favilla
into believable elements of fiction. Furthermore, in "The Model
Daughter" the antecedent action is made clear so that the encounter between Fidelia, the model daughter, and the woman
who wants her to "see" her son—complete with dialogue—is un-
derstandable. Fidelia, by being given words to utter and by being given a personality as well as a name, certainly is more than a
mere type. And the same is true of Irus, "The Frugal, Retired
Man" (No. 264), who is revealed through a rapid biographical
survey that gives the details of an individual: "*Irus*, tho' he is now
turned fifty, has not appeared in the World, in his real Character,
since five and twenty, at which Age he ran out a small Patrimony,

and spent some Time after with Rakes who had lived upon him
. . ." (*Spectator,* II, 527). Mr. Spectator's specific portrait of the
man, with the particulars of where he lives, makes the reader
more aware of the reality of the situation and the man.

The brightest example of the "individual" Characters, however, must surely be Addison's Character of Will Wimble, which
is *Spectator* No. 108. The letter device is again used, as is the brief
biographical survey of the individual, but the whole is couched in
a narrative episode. Mr. Spectator and Sir Roger are walking in
the country when a messenger arrives with a letter from Will
Wimble that announces his intention to visit in order to "see how
the Perch bite in the *Black River*" (*Spectator,* I, 446). This allows
the narrator, Mr. Spectator, to introduce his biographical sketch
of Will, as told by Sir Roger. Then the narrative continues: "Sir
ROGER was proceeding in the Character of him, when we saw
him make up to us, with two or three Hazle-twigs in his Hand that
he had cut in Sir ROGER's Woods, as he came through them, in
his Way to the House" (*Spectator,* I, 447-48). What follows is a
description of Will in action, as they are called by the bell to din-
ner and as they withdraw to Mr. Spectator's room afterwards.
Only at this point does Mr. Spectator tie together the actions with
what has been the theme of the whole: "*Will Wimble*'s is the Case
of many a younger Brother of a great Family, who had rather see
their Children starve like Gentlemen, than thrive in a Trade or
Profession that is beneath their Quality" (*Spectator,* I, 448). The
whole episode is thus unified, cleverly linked in its various parts,
and "individual" in its import. There is an aspect of reality here
that is far beyond what is evident in the old Characters: the techniques are more elastic, and the result is a form with great narrative possibilities.

The classification of the Characters, as they represent varying
degrees of typicality and individuality, makes it clear that the
authors of the *Spectator* were not satisfied with following the
strict Theophrastan methods and that in their subject matter and
techniques of handling the material they did much to elasticize

the form. In fact, in the "individual" Characters particularly, the Character is not, as Melvin R. Watson claims, "largely functional," for the individuals can well stand on their merits.[26] One can detect a development toward short narrative fiction—though not a chronological movement—in such areas as the emphasis on realistic details, the interaction of two or more characters whose spoken words and dialogue are sometimes recorded, the variety of style, which abandons in the majority of cases the anaphora of Hall and Overbury, the increasingly logical organization of thought, and the effort to concentrate less on numerous aspects of a type and more on the primary traits of a named person. Even when types are presented, Mr. Spectator uses every trick at hand to make the reader think that a real person is meant. Gwendolen Murphy found the effect of the old Characters to be that "of a string of adjectives rather than of a reasoned narrative,"[27] but in the hands of Addison, Steele, Hughes, and Budgell—and with the influence of La Bruyère—this is simply not the case. In the *Spectator*, the Character often approaches what Benjamin Boyce says the best Character must have: "it represents a class, yet it must seem to possess the reality of a flesh-and-blood individual; it pleases by graphic detail and illuminates by hints, yet it must not be endangered by the merely local and temporary."[28] The Character in the *Spectator* is indeed a protean form.

3

The Fable

Fables were the first pieces of Wit that made their appearance in the World, and have been still highly valued, not only in times of the greatest Simplicity, but among the most polite Ages of Mankind.

—Mr. Spectator, *Spectator* No. 183

Reading the stories in the *Spectator,* one might puzzle over the rather summary fashion in which many of them are treated, the frequent disregard for character development, and the labored insistence on the apparent truth of the tale being told. Addison and Steele are often more concerned with the theme itself than with development of dialogue and characterization, although the preceding study of the Character shows that this is not as pervasive as is often thought. The fable in the *Spectator* is nevertheless normally used, primarily in the hands of Addison, to further his moral teachings, however much the form, as Melvin R. Watson notes, "shows the effect of his peculiar ability to infuse new life into an ancient, dessicated [*sic*] form."[1]

That Addison was quite aware of the power of fiction, and particularly the fable, to exert a social influence is clear. In *Spectator* No. 512 he mentions the importance of the fable as the least shocking means of giving advice because (1) upon the reading of a fable we are made to believe we advise ourselves and (2) the moral insinuates itself imperceptibly and, therefore, we are taught by surprise and become wiser and better unawares (*Spectator*, IV, 318). The value of the fable in his scheme lies mainly in the fact that it forces the reader to become a participant—everything appears to be a discovery of his own. At this point in No. 512 Addison, quite typically, tells a fable to illustrate his point that instruction and delight are products of the fable. Casually, Mr. Spectator comments that "there is a pretty Instance of this Nature in a *Turkish* Tale, which I do not like the worse for that little Oriental Extravagance which is mixed with it" (*Spectator*, IV, 318). The fable pertains to Sultan Mahmoud, who has, through perpetual war, brought ruin to his dominion. A "Dervise," who pretends to know the language of birds, is sent by the Sultan to overhear the conversation between two owls. One of the owls, it is reported, hails the Sultan with the words "*God grant a long Life to Sultan* Mahmoud! *whilst he reigns over us we shall never want ruined Villages.*" The Sultan is awakened to the needs of his country and immediately begins to rebuild the villages out of the ruins (*Spectator*, IV, 318–19).[2]

In the *Spectator* twenty-three fables are either mentioned, referred to briefly, or related in an extended fashion—all except five by Joseph Addison. They may be classified as oriental or eastern fables, traditional (usually animal) fables, and allegorical fables. There is some confusion about the meaning of the term "fable," for in No. 55 Addison uses it synonymously with "allegory"; but Dr. Johnson's definition in his *Life of Gay* is a good guide: "A Fable or Apologue . . . seems to be in its genuine state a narrative in which beings irrational, and sometimes inanimate . . . are for the purpose of moral instruction feigned to act and speak with human interests and passions."[3] As with Johnson's Gay, this description does not always conform; Addison's "fable" sometimes is a tale of abstracted "allegory" or a little "Oriental Extravagance." There is often no attempt to keep the various types separate. When Addison discusses the antiquity and development of the fable in *Spectator* No. 183, for example, he characteristically lumps together Aesop, Homer, and Edmund Spenser and concludes with what is certainly a pure allegory of pleasure and pain.[4] "Fables," says Addison, "were the first pieces of Wit that made their appearance in the World, and have been still highly valued, not only in times of the greatest Simplicity, but among the most polite Ages of Mankind" (*Spectator,* II, 219).

Aside from the oriental fable already mentioned, "The Visier Who Understood the Language of Birds" (No. 512), Addison wrote three other so-called fables with the unmistakable fragrance of the mysterious East. As "The Visier" caps Addison's point about the value of fables, so likewise "The Sultan's Exercise" (No. 195), "The Pearl Swallowed by an Oyster" (No. 293), and "Alnaschar, the Persian Glass-merchant" (No. 535) drive home the central idea of a particular essay with devastating simplicity. Whether Addison uses the eastern fable to whet the imagination of his audience (as he does in No. 193 by beginning his reflections with "The Sultan's Exercise") or as an imagistic ornament for his thoughts (as is the case with Nos. 293 and 535, where the fables occur at the conclusion of an essay), the function is didactic. He turns strictly imaginative literature into philosophic and moralistic channels.

Accordingly, when he relates these oriental fables, Mr. Spectator does not attempt to conceal their function. Near the end of No. 535, which is devoted to the subject of foolish Hope, the narrator formally introduces the fable about Alnaschar and makes it plain that it is not merely amusement:

> The Fable has in it such a wild, but natural, Simplicity, that I question not but my Reader will be as much pleased with it as I have been, and that he will consider himself, if he reflects on the several Amusements of Hope which have sometimes passed in his Mind, as a near Relation to the *Persian* Glass-Man. (*Spectator,* IV, 410)

The fable (faithfully following the *Thousand and One Nights* original) tells of Alnaschar's inheriting 100 Drachmas, his buying bottles and expensive glass with it, placing all this in a basket to sell at retail prices on the streets, his daydreaming about his mounting riches, and his kicking over the basket in his sleep and breaking everything into ten thousand pieces. With the fable the essay on Hope ends; no additional comment is offered or needed.

Addison's method in No. 293 is the same. The introduction is brief but formal: "Since on this Subject I have already admitted several Quotations which have occurred to my Memory upon writing this Paper, I will conclude it with a little *Persian* Fable." Mr. Spectator then presents the fable in a summary fashion in which at regular intervals he makes evident the ancient authority of his example:

> A Drop of Water fell out of a Cloud into the Sea, and finding it self lost in such an Immensity of fluid Matter, broke out into the following Reflection: "Alas! What an inconsiderable Creature am I in this prodigious Ocean of Waters; My Existence is of no Concern to the Universe, I am reduced to a kind of nothing, and am less than the least of the Works of God." It so happened, that an Oyster, which lay in the neighbourhood of this Drop, chanced to gape and swallow it up in the midst of this his humble Soliloquy. The Drop, says the Fable, lay a great while hardning in the Shell, 'till by degrees it was ripen'd into a Pearl, which falling into the Hands of a Diver, after a long Series of Adventures, is at present that famous Pearl which is fixed on the Top of the *Persian* Diadem. (*Spectator*, III, 46) [5]

Mr. Spectator, the storyteller par excellence, thus confronts the reader with a once-upon-a-time "so the fable says" story. This method of manipulating the material he had at his disposal permits Addison to buttress the didactic purpose and to enhance the fictional image of Mr. Spectator as the putative author and narrator of the *Spectator* papers.

In addition to the oriental fables, there are sixteen fables in the *Spectator*, either mentioned or told more fully, that are not allegorical; these traditional fables normally concern animals or inanimate objects. Although their being referred to knowingly says a great deal about the authors' interest in the fable as an instrument of delight and instruction, eight of the sixteen are nevertheless mentioned so briefly and with so little elaboration that analysis is not called for.[6] Apparently Mr. Spectator assumes that brief mention is enough to tap the "deep well" of the reader's knowledge. The eight remaining fables all serve a largely functional purpose and are not presented merely for the sake of the story. Sometimes the fable is incorporated into the narrative framework, but oftentimes it is used where Mr. Spectator's presence is not felt as a part of a formal exposition or essay.

Steele's "The Lion and the Man" (No. 11) is successfully presented in a narrative context. The fable is used to accentuate the effect of the piece as a whole, and Steele does not change the fable in any way, except to shorten it, from what it was in Aesop.[7] While it illustrates the point of the essay, an excellent method is employed to integrate it into the narrative. Arietta, whom Mr. Spectator is visiting, tells the fable in order to counteract the ideas of another visitor, a commonplace talker about constancy in love. After his lengthy discourse, Arietta turns to him and says:

> But your Quotations put me in Mind of the Fable of the Lion and the Man. The Man walking with that noble Animal, showed him, in the Ostentation of Human Superiority, a Sign of a Man killing a Lion. Upon which the Lion said very justly, *We Lions are none of us Painters, else we could show a hundred Men killed by Lions, for one Lion killed by a Man.* (*Spectator*, I, 48–49)

Then the idea of the fable is immediately applied to the situation: "You Men are Writers, and can represent us Women as Unbecoming as you please in your Works, while we are unable to return the Injury" (*Spectator*, I, 49). Steele very smoothly works the fable into the conversation between two people, and it is not cumbersome since he condenses it economically into two sentences.

The use of the fable for didactic purposes is also illustrated in Addison's "The Old Man and His Two Wives" (No. 34), which hardly amounts to more than brief mention of Aesop's fable. The piece is a narrative account by Mr. Spectator of a discussion by a group of members of the Club about the success of the *Spectator*.

Sir Roger suggests that he leave fox-hunters alone, and Captain Sentry suggests that he leave the Army out of it. Mr. Spectator is perplexed:

> By this Time I found every Subject of my Speculations was taken away from me by one or other of the Club; and began to think my self in the Condition of the good Man that had one Wife who took a Dislike to his grey Hairs, and another to his black, till by their picking out what each of them had an Aversion to, they left his Head altogether bald and naked. (*Spectator*, I, 143)

Oftentimes, however, the fable is presented formally as a part of an essay that has no narrative qualities, in answer to a correspondent's letter, or enclosed in a letter from a reader. They are always short and illustrative of the central idea of the particular issue. As universal examples geared to the common man's level, these fables are used as a part of an essay: Addison's "The Frogs and the Boys" (No. 23), "The Mole" (No. 124), "The Woman Who Broke Her Looking Glass" (No. 451), and "Pandora's Box" (No. 471). The method of handling in No. 23 will suffice to show his technique in all four of these fables. In No. 23 Mr. Spectator's central idea is that an indiscreet man, who hurts friends and foes indifferently, is more injurious than an ill-natured man who attacks only his enemies. Notice the formal manner in which he then introduces his fable to illustrate his point:

> I cannot forbear, on this occasion, transcribing a Fable out of Sir *Roger L'Estrange*, which accidentally lies before me. "A Company of Waggish Boys were watching of Frogs at the side of a Pond, and still as any of 'em put up their Heads, they'd be pelting them down again with Stones. *Children* (says one of the Frogs) *you never consider that though this may be Play to you, 'tis Death to us.*" (*Spectator*, I, 100)

In No. 25 Mr. Spectator uses the fable "Of Jupiter and the Countryman" to answer the letter from the valetudinarian just as Arietta had used a fable to answer her tormenter in No. 11.

Again there is no attempt to disguise the functional purpose of
the form: "In answer to the Gentleman . . . I shall tell him a short
Fable" (*Spectator*, I, 108). Then follows a close summary of
Aesop's fable, which concludes the selection and effectively brings
the central idea full circle without the reader's feeling preached
at. In No. 246 a correspondent also employs the device of briefly
mentioning a fable of "Earth and Plants," also from Aesop, to
illustrate his thoughts. The letter condemns mothers who hurriedly turn a child over for another to nurse, because

> "like *Aesop's* Earth, which would not nurse the Plant of another
> Ground, altho' never so much improved, by Reason that Plant
> was not of its own Production."

" 'And since another's Child is no more natural to a Nurse than a
Plant to a strange and different Ground' " the correspondent asks,
" 'how can it be supposed that the Child should thrive?' " (*Spectator*, II, 455).

Clearly, then, the important point is not how much Addison
used the fable in the *Spectator,* but what he did with the material,
which, as noted, is principally taken from Aesop. He turned the
imaginative literature into common moralistic and philosophic
channels, and in so doing helped immensely to create a taste for
fiction as an acceptable form of literature among the rank and
file.[8] In the *Spectator* itself, Mr. Spectator makes the form work
for him in both his narrative episodes and in his essays, showing
once again his great gift of infusing new life into an ancient, desic-
cated form.

But Addison was not content, as with the Character, to write
only one kind of fable or to cling to one approach. The "new life"
had to be instilled in a variety of ways, and another means was
through allegory. Even though "Fables were the first pieces of
Wit that made their appearance in the World," Addison looked
for inspiration as well to Boileau and La Fontaine, "who by this
way of Writing is come more into Vogue than any other Author

of our Times" (*Spectator*, II, 220). Thus Addison in No. 183 writes an original allegorical fable of "Pleasure and Pain," a carefully organized story of how Pleasure, the daughter of Happiness, and Pain, the son of Misery, came to marry on Earth, halfway between Heaven and Hell: *"By this means it is that we find Pleasure and Pain are such constant Yoke-fellows, and that they either make their Visits together, or are never far asunder"* (*Spectator*, II, 223). His use of allegory in the fable is also demonstrated in "A Heathen Fable Relating to Prayers" (No. 391), which is an expansion of an episode in Thomas Brown's translation of Lucian's *Icaromenippus: or, a Voyage to Heaven* (*Spectator*, III, 468, 468 *n*). And Addison's "Of Luxury and Avarice" (No. 55), furthermore, is presented as an allegorical example of how love of pleasure or fear of want dominate men's lives; No. 55 is quite similar in method and general subject matter to his "Pleasure and Pain" fable. There is the storybook introduction ("There were two very powerful Tyrants engaged . . .") followed by a biographical survey of the characters and the introduction of the conflict, which in turn illustrates a universal truth. In "Of Luxury and Avarice" this truth is stated, as usual, in a concentrated, epigrammatic concluding sentence that ties the whole narrative together: "To which I shall only add, that since the discarding of the Counsellors above mentioned, *Avarice* supplies *Luxury* in the room of *Plenty*, as *Luxury* Prompts *Avarice* in the place of *Poverty*" (*Spectator*, I, 236).

The fable in the *Spectator* is used extensively—although it is sometimes only in the form of an allusion to a well-known fable or is oftentimes briefly presented in a mere three or four sentences—to promote the didactic purpose in an entertaining manner. Mr. Spectator varies his methods, and his approach is seldom predictable; the subject matter ranges from the inanimate to the animate, from the irrational to the abstract. What the mole and the frog do not attract in a reader, perhaps Pleasure, Avarice, Luxury, and Plenty in their Englished world will. Though the fable is more often than not an abbreviation of a longer original, its use in the

Spectator reveals an extension of its powers to please "the most universally . . . in whatsoever Shape it appears" (*Spectator*, IV, 317).

4

The Dream Vision-Cum-Allegory

. . . While I dissolve
The Mists and Films that mortal Eyes involve:
Purge from your sight the Dross. . . .
—Virgil, *Aeneid*, 2.604–06 (Dryden)
Motto for *Spectator* No. 159

"Had I printed every one that came to my Hands," reflected Mr. Spectator in No. 524, "my Book of Speculations would have been little else but a Book of Visions" (*Spectator*, IV, 365). It was, to be sure, a form patently suited to the purposes of his daily periodical; the vision provided easy entry into amusing, mysterious, adventuresome realms of extraordinary delight and a welcome opportunity to meet the potentates of the virtues and vices lying at the very root of human life. As Addison noted on one occasion, the dream vision falls "in with the Taste of all my popular Readers, and amuse[s] the Imaginations of those who are more profound" (*Spectator*, IV, 365). It is not, therefore, surprising that seventeen dream visions with allegorical overtones appear in the *Spectator;* in fact, Addison's comment on the form's popularity with his readers might have led us to anticipate more. Apparently both he and his so-called correspondents took too seriously his remedy for the numerous visions that flooded his desk: "To prevent this Inundation of Dreams . . . I shall apply to all Dreamers of Dreams, the Advice which *Epictetus* has couched after his manner . . . *Never tell thy Dreams . . . for tho' thou thy self may'st take a Pleasure in telling thy Dream, another will take no Pleasure in hearing it"* (*Spectator,* IV, 365).

As with the fable, the area of the dream vision-cum-allegory is primarily Addison's; Steele ventured into this type of story only twice (Nos. 392 and 514), though on one occasion he draws in allegorical form, via the letter technique, an elaborate parallel between gardening and education (No. 455).[1] Generally, there are three reasons for writing various dream visions: political, literary, and moral. But also occasionally one can detect an element of Horatian satire.[2] Addison and Steele were particularly adept at ridiculing wrong out of fashion, and this trait carries over even into the fictional dream visions. They could, like Chaucer, "turne us every dreem to gode!"

The basic structure of the dream visions varies little, even though the tenor of the theme may be political, literary, or moral. An ordinary mortal, either Mr. Spectator or Will Honeycomb, or some other man from the streets of London, always envisions himself in contact with a world that is usually inhabited by personifications of the virtues and vices. It is at once real and much more than real, because it is a world in concentrated miniature. The mortal is often conducted on a tour of the region by a friendly guide, who does not, however, prevent his being tempted, endangered, or terrified before his final recognition of the "truth," which usually wakes him up. The scene of the encounter in the dream visions of the *Spectator* is ordinarily a plain, a green woods, or an expanse of road leading to a palace or a building of some description: for example, in No. 3 there is a "Great Hall"; in No. 56 there is "a long Space under a hollow Mountain . . . [surrounded by] a thick Forest made up of Bushes, Brambles, and pointed Thorns"; in No. 63 there is "nothing in the Fields, the Woods, and the Rivers, that appeared natural"; in No. 83 there is "a long spacious Gallery"; in No. 301 there is "a large valley divided by a River of the purest Water"; in No. 460 Mr. Spectator is "transported to a Hill, green, flowery, and of an easy Ascent," and so on. In these surroundings one confronts lions that are but walking shadows, ladies languishing on creek banks in flowing robes, women with names like Solitude—or even Publick Credit—sitting on thrones of glory, and men winding and turning in labyrinthine despair. With the exception of Marraton and Yaratilda in No. 56, all the characters are obvious personifications of abstract ideas, real elements of government and literature, and concrete objects. The characters are not flesh and blood; rather, they are representative people for a paper designed to entertain, and hopfully to instruct, a man drinking cocoa for half an hour at Will's or St. James's. Such allegory prescribes the direction of a critic's commentary and so restricts its freedom; the dream visions in the *Spectator* are primarily and foremost a translation of ideas into images.[3]

The typical method employed by the authors to introduce the dream visions into the context of the essay is simple. The narrator, or essayist, is usually reading, preferably from a classical author such as Herodotus or Homer, or thinking about an idea derived from a discussion or a sermon heard during the day; upon going to sleep or drifting into reverie, he dreams a dream that embodies the ideas that theoretically stimulated him. A typical example is No. 524, where the narrator, a man from Glasgow, had heard a cracking fire-and-brimstone (Presbyterian) sermon on the reasonableness of virtue, and that night, he says, " 'Methought I was just awoke out of a Sleep, that I could never remember the beginning of; the Place where I found my self to be was a wide and spacious Plain . . .' " (*Spectator*, IV, 366).[4] A variation of this technique is illustrated in No. 463:

> I was lately entertaining my self with comparing *Homer*'s Ballance, in which *Jupiter* is represented as weighing the Fates of *Hector* and *Achilles*, with a Passage of *Virgil*, wherein that Deity is introduced as weighing the Fates of *Turnus* and *Aeneas*. I then considered, how the same way of thinking prevailed in the Eastern Parts of the World, as in those noble Passages of

Scripture. . . . These several amusing Thoughts having taken Possession of my Mind some time before I went to sleep, and mingling themselves with my ordinary Ideas, raised in my Imagination a very odd kind of Vision. (*Spectator*, IV, 134–35)

The closing of the dream visions is always explained in physical terms that relate to some action within the dream itself. The narrator has accomplished his task and straightened out the entangling problem posed by the dream world, and the physical return to reality indicates an awakening to the truth of the dream message or the arrival at the fixed destination. In "Truth and False Wit" (No. 63), for instance, Mr. Spectator at last

was very much awed and delighted with the Appearance of the God of *Wit;* there was something so amiable and yet so piercing in his Looks, as inspired me at once with Love and Terrour. As I was gazing on him to my unspeakable Joy, he took a Quiver of Arrows from his Shoulder, in order to make me a Present of it, but as I was reaching out my Hand to receive it of him, I knocked it against a Chair, and by that means awaked. (*Spectator*, I, 274)

Another similar, typical way of closing the dream vision—and one that illustrates the extent to which Addison varies the basic pattern—is the conclusion to "Dissection of a Coquet's Heart" (No. 281):

As we were admiring this *Phaenomenon*, and standing round the Heart in a Circle, it gave a most prodigious Sigh or rather Crack, and dispersed all at once in Smoke and Vapour. This imaginary Noise, which methoughts was louder than the burst of a Cannon, produced such a violent Shake in my Brain, that it dissipated the Fumes of Sleep, and left me in an instant broad awake. (*Spectator*, II, 597)

Such employment of movement or noise within the dream vision itself, signifying the shock of recognition, to signal the end of the reverie is neither old nor new, but it is effective in its simplicity and practicality. It images an experience as it solidifies the abstract, often obtuse reaches of man's mental journeys.

One of the *Spectator's* few sallies into the political arena occurs in "Decay of Publick Credit" (No. 3), the only strictly politically oriented dream vision and one that has satirical overtones. Coming at the very beginning of the *Spectator* it affords an excellent opportunity to notice techniques. "Decay of Publick Credit" begins in much the same way as Chaucer's poetic dreams; the reflection of the day calls up a dream at night. Like Walter Mitty's, Mr. Spectator's real world is fused into imaginative dream:

> The Thoughts of the Day gave my Mind Employment for the whole Night, so that I fell insensibly into a kind of Methodical Dream, which dispos'd all my Contemplations into a Vision or Allegory, or what else the Reader shall please to call it. (*Spectator*, I, 14)

The purpose of the vision is explicitly to illustrate, first of all, the thesis that Addison advances in the second sentence of the essay: "[Walking by the Bank] revived in my Memory the many Discourses which I had both read and heard concerning the Decay of Publick Credit, with the Methods of restoring it, and which, in my Opinion, have always been defective, because they have always been made with an Eye to separate Interests, and Party Principles" (*Spectator*, I, 14).

After Mr. Spectator enters the Great Hall of his dream, Addison immediately introduces the reader to the central figure, Publick Credit, and gives a clear view of the setting. He cannot be too specific in describing Publick Credit (she must remain all-embracing), but enough individualism is allotted her to distinguish her from the merely female; she is "infinitely timorous in all her Behavior" as well as "a beautiful Virgin." Addison places this person in a concretely described setting: "I saw," says Mr. Spectator,

> towards the Upper-end of the Hall, a beautiful Virgin, seated on a Throne of Gold. Her name (as they told me) was *Publick*

Credit. The Walls, instead of being adorned with Pictures and Maps, were hung with many Acts of Parliament written in Golden Letters. At the Upper-end of the Hall was the *Magna Charta,* with the Act of Uniformity on the right Hand, and the Act of Toleration on the left. At the Lower-end of the Hall was the Act of Settlement, which was placed full in the Eye of the Virgin that sat upon the Throne. Both the Sides of the Hall were covered with such Acts. . . . (*Spectator,* I, 15)

Addison apparently tries to emphasize the credibility of his chief character by saturating the mind of the reader with exact dimensions of the locale. Furthermore, with setting and character outlined, Addison loses no time in introducing the conflict (protecting the Hall and its contents from enemies), which is followed by action directly related (enemies enter) and a resolution of the conflict (Liberty, Moderation, and the Spirit of Great Britain drive them off). There is unity of action and mood, therefore, which the limited action and the few characters in a particular setting achieve. The ingredients for the short story are there.

But what about the narrator, Mr. Spectator, and his obviously important role in the story? As might be expected, he is self-conscious, more so here at the beginning of the *Spectator* than he is later on when justification is not so important. He tries to explain, for example, how he knows what he knows: "She was likewise (as I afterwards found) a greater Valetudinarian than any I had ever met with . . ." (*Spectator,* I, 15). Also the narrator attempts to convey the impression that he is being frank and revealing all he knows (establishing credibility)—one of the attacking couples, the third, was the Genius of a Common-Wealth and "a young Man of about twenty two Years of Age, whose Name I could not learn" (*Spectator,* I, 16). Later on, the artificiality of this device becomes apparent when Addison too neatly balances this bad couple with the third group of "amiable Phantoms," who are "a Person whom I had never seen, with the Genius of *Great Britain*" (*Spectator,* I, 17). Addison makes a valiant attempt to give his narrator some degree of credibility, some human traits and limitations that his audience can identify with, but he fails in this early dream vision because such qualities of credibility are not necessary in a narrator who is supposedly *dreaming* and because his narrative techniques are too finely drawn. If a storyteller makes a camel go through the eye of a needle, it is after all unnecessary to add that it is a very thin camel. Addison might judiciously have applied to this story his advice about operas: "Shadows and Realities ought not to be mix'd together in the same Piece . . ." (*Spectator*, I, 23). Mr. Spectator, at this stage attempting to establish his credibility as an essayist and his credibility as a narrator, is not altogether capable of handling this double burden.

Besides this initial dream vision, which is the only one that can be classified as "political," there are four "literary" ones and twelve "moral" visions. The four so-called literary dream visions are "Marraton and Yaratilda" (No. 56), which is not allegorical, "Truth and False Wit" (No. 63), "Vision of the Painters" (No. 83), and "The Seasons" (No. 425). Since they happen to occur, except for No. 425, as the next three visions after "Publick Credit," they provide an opportunity to observe if Mr. Spectator improves as a fictional narrator in the course of the first three months of the *Spectator*. One can see, furthermore, how Addison conceals more effectively than in No. 3 the hand of the artist at work.

Spectator No. 56 begins with a discussion by Mr. Spectator, the essayist, about the American Indian belief that all things have souls, a belief that he considers no more preposterous than what some European philosophers have said. At this point he lets it be known that he intends to illustrate his point with a story, which he accounts for in his usual rather stilted manner:

> A Friend of mine, whom I have formerly mentioned, prevailed upon one of the Interpreters of the *Indian* Kings, to enquire of them, if possible, what Tradition they have among them of this Matter: Which, as well as he could learn by those many Questions which he asked them at several Times, was in Substance as follows. (*Spectator*, I, 237)

The account of Marraton's visionary journey into the Confines of the World of Spirits is, contrary to the method in "Publick Credit," narrated in a much less self-conscious manner. In fact, Mr. Spectator tells the story mainly in the manner in which he would have heard it, third-person narrative, and he does not have to justify all his information. And when Mr. Spectator does step into the story, Addison here conceals his art with art that effects a smooth transition from the opening conflicts with visionary lions, thorns, and trees to the closing attempts to reach Yaratilda:

> I should have told my Reader, that this *Indian* had been former-ly married to one of the greatest Beauties of his Country, by whom he had several Children. This Couple were so famous for their Love and Constancy to one another, that the *Indians* to this Day, when they give a married Man Joy of his Wife, wish that they may live together like *Marraton* and *Yaratilda*. *Marraton* had not stood long by the Fisherman when he saw the Shadow of his beloved *Yaratilda*. . . . (*Spectator*, I, 239)

When he reaches Yaratilda, she points out to Marraton the home she has waiting for him and the children "that they might here-after all of them meet together in this happy Place" (*Spectator*, I, 240). The moral lesson is implied, but Mr. Spectator does not be-labor it. In fact, Richard Hurd's comment about the techniques and methods of this vision, made in his 1811 edition of Addison's works, is still applicable today: "All the graces of imagination, are here joined with all the light and lustre of expression: but it was not for nothing (as the concluding moral shews) that so much wit and elegance was employed on this subject."[5] The piece is a genuine improvement over Addison's first dream vision.

Addison's "Truth and False Wit" (No. 63) serves as an illustra-tive capstone for his previous extended discussion of Wit. The story has a beginning, a middle, and an end that are well co-ordinated with the schematic purpose. Here Mr. Spectator, again the first-person narrator and participant, is not overly anxious to defend his position, and he succeeds as a character. Although he meets the Goddess of Falsehood and other such beings, the story is more than a genealogical prose chart; and, even though the allegorical characters are incapable of humanity and individuality as such, the abstractions are placed in a setting and a scene that is made real on its own terms. We may not know the dimensions of the place or the directions of things in relation to the needs of this world—as Addison related in No. 3—but in this dream vision he artistically uses Mr. Spectator to lure the reader into the sensual world of dream.

"Truth and False Wit" may be read, perhaps should be read, not simply for the allegory but for the fantasy of the plot. One is carried by Mr. Spectator from the world of reality to a place of enchantment. He offers no apologies for his presence, and the details are set forth with confidence, without begging the question of knowledge. Particularly noteworthy is the narrator's imagistic language, which almost completely surrounds the reader's senses. Everything in the fields, woods, and rivers appeals to the sense of sight, smell, or sound: to the sense of sight in "Several of the Trees blossom'd in Leaf-Gold, some of them produced Bone-Lace, and some of them precious Stones"; to the sense of smell in his description of the flowers that "perfumed the Air"; and to the sense of sound in

> The Fountains bubbled in an Opera Tune, and were filled with Stags, Wild-Boars and Mermaids, that lived among the Waters, at the same time that Dolphins and several kinds of Fish played upon the Banks, or took their Pastime in the Meadows. The Birds had many of them Golden Beaks, and human Voices. (*Spectator,* I, 271)

For these reasons, Addison's fictional techniques of style and narration, as well as unity and tone, are definite reminders that he was writing a story that was consciously *made* and artistically shaped.

In No. 83 Mr. Spectator relates another literary dream vision, which is brought on by his visits to the art galleries on rainy days.

In the preface—not in the vision itself—he asks the reader not to consider it as a finished story:

> I was some Weeks ago in a Course of these Diversions, which had taken such an entire Possession of my Imagination, that they formed in it a short Morning's Dream, which I shall communicate to my Reader, rather as the first Sketch and Outlines of a Vision, than as a finished Piece. (*Spectator*, I, 354)

Indeed, the piece is more important for its allegory than for the narrative element and character interaction. It is a vehicle on which to place his satirical remarks about modern painting. After entering the "spacious Gallery, which had one side covered with Pieces of all the Famous Painters who are now living, and the other with the Works of the greatest Masters that are dead," Mr. Spectator proceeds to describe the various people and their reactions to the paintings. "On the side of the *Living*," Mr. Spectator notes with the cool detachment of a satirist,

> I saw several Persons busy in Drawing, Colouring, and Designing. On the side of the *Dead* Painters, I could not discover more than one Person at Work, who was exceeding slow in his Motions, and wonderfully nice in his Touches. (*Spectator*, I, 354)

The dream vision here is a story type handled in a manner that emphasizes the allegorical satire and is an appropriate form for Addison's presentation of a microcosmic, exaggerated illustration of the real world's taste in one area of the fine arts. It enlivens morality with wit in the best Addisonian tradition.

In "The Seasons" (No. 425), a literary dream vision of which the specific author is not known, the technique of handling the material and the allegorical depiction of the seasons, which the narrator meets in his dream, are not developed in a significantly different manner. The narrator is varied (a correspondent), but the method of developing the story is the same. There is, however, a more conscious effort to instill or prepare for the tone of the vision in the essayistic preface, which concerns man's universal desire to go into his garden for reflection after a hot sultry day. The mood is lazy, peaceful, and serene:

> "The Moon shone bright, and seem'd then most agreeably to supply the Place of the Sun, obliging me with as much Light as was necessary to discover a thousand pleasing Objects, and at the same Time divested of all Power of Heat. The Reflection of it in the Water, the Fanning of the Wind rustling on the Leaves, the Singing of the Thrush and Nightingale, and the Coolness of the Walks, all conspired to make me lay aside all displeasing Thoughts, and brought me into such a Tranquility of Mind, as is I believe the next Happiness to that of hereafter. In this sweet Retirement, I naturally fell into the Repetition of some Lines of a Poem of *Milton's*, which he entitles *Il Penseroso*, the Ideas of which were exquisitely suited to my present Wandrings of Thought. . . ." (*Spectator*, III, 593)

This kind of prologue prepares the reader for the forthcoming drama and differing scenes of the revolution of the year. The subject of the seasons advancing before the observer of course gives the dream a built-in organization that in the conclusion comes full circle.

The twelve dream visions written expressly for moral purposes include Addison's "The Vision of Mirzah" (No. 159), "Dissection of a Beau's Head (No. 275), "Dissection of a Coquet's Heart" (No. 281), Budgell's "Love and Old Age" (No. 301), Steele's "Transformation of Fidelio into a Looking-Glass" (No. 392), Parnell's "The Paradise of Fools" (No. 460), Addison's "The Golden Scales" (No. 463), "The Modern Women of Hensberg" (No. 499), Parnell's "The Grotto of Grief" (No. 501), Addison's "A Sale of London Women" (No. 511), Steele's "A Vision of Mt. Parnassus" (No. 514), and "Heavenly and Worldly Wisdom" (No. 524), by an unknown author. All these dream visions-cum-allegory have a more overtly didactic purpose than the political and literary ones, and they normally contain a strong religious-philosophical theme of social import designed to influence the Englishman at the start of the Age of Enlightenment to lead the good life, to follow the road less traveled.

"The Vision of Mirzah" (No. 159) is probably the best known and is certainly the most frequently anthologized short story in the *Spectator*. It gives a picture of life, and, although various sources have been suggested, Donald F. Bond comments that "the symbolism is so simple and effective that no printed source need be assumed" (*Spectator*, II, 121*n*). The story itself—enveloping as it does a naive, simple allegory—employs a first-person narrator who encounters the Genius of the Rock, who in turn acts as an interpreter of the scene. The structure is balanced and tightly knit; at the beginning the narrator ascends "the high Hills of *Bagdat*," and in the conclusion the reader is neatly returned to this location after the journey into the depths of the mind:

> "I turned about to address my self to him a second time, but I found that he had left me; I then turned again to the Vision which I had been so long contemplating, but instead of the rolling Tide, the arched Bridge, and the happy Islands, I saw nothing but the long hollow Valley of *Bagdat*, with Oxen, Sheep, and Camels, grazing upon the Sides of it." (*Spectator*, II, 126)

The scene is static—the two stand on a high place and describe the panorama before them (the wide valley, the gulf spanned by a bridge, and the procession of people over the bridge), and it is towards the situation they see, the image before their eyes, that everything is focused.

Since the allegory of life is the thing, Addison had to employ some method that would make this point clear to his broad reading public without having to rely again (he was always searching for variety) on Mr. Spectator to convey the interpretation after the conclusion of the story. He uses a simple but effective technique within the story: the real-life narrator describes the literal level of the plot, and the visionary personified abstraction takes an active role by explaining to the narrator in a person-to-person manner the symbolic level of the episode. The literal image of the abstract world is explained step by step in moral or religious terms. The reader therefore is forced to move back and forth from the literal to a symbolic mode of thinking, as if Addison is teaching the reader how to make such associations from specific pedestrian incidents in life. Dialogue is the device that accomplishes this purpose:

> "He then led me to the highest Pinnacle of the Rock, and placing me on the Top of it, Cast thy Eyes Eastward, said he, and tell me what thou seest. I see, said I, a huge Valley and a prodigious Tide of Water rolling through it. The Valley that thou seest, said he, is the Vale of Misery, and the Tide of Water that thou seest is Part of the great Tide of Eternity. What is the Reason, said I, that the Tide I see rises out of a thick Mist at one End, and again loses it self in a thick Mist at the other? What thou seest, said he, is that Portion of Eternity which is called Time, measured out by the Sun, and reaching from the Beginning of the World to its Consummation. Examine now, said he, this Sea that is thus bounded with Darkness at both Ends, and tell me what thou discoverest in it. I see a Bridge, said I, standing in the Midst of the Tide. The Bridge thou seest, said he, is humane Life. . . ." (*Spectator*, II, 123)

Such judicious use of fictional techniques to advance the purpose of his essay and to frame a simple story that has since been admired by generations is no small evidence of how effective short fiction can be. The mixing in of some oriental material and the fiction of its being an old, newly discovered manuscript from Grand Cairo also varies the tenor of this moral dream vision and gives it a freshness that still remains.

Two of the moral dream visions combine the same theme, are a part of the same dream, and occur in two separate issues of the *Spectator*. They provide the continued serial effect of the cumulative episode, which is always complete but always to be added to. In "Dissection of a Beau's Head" (No. 275) and "Dissection of a Coquet's Heart" (No. 281), Addison continues to employ the narrator to present a detached view of the social world of Lon-

don. He adopts, according to Bond, "an original framework for
driving home his meaning" and combines "a telling analysis of
fashionable frivolity with a neat and graphic incident" (*Spectator,*
I, lx). The graphic incident in the pieces is the dissection of the
head and the heart of the beau and coquet and is allegory based
on metonymy. The real objects are seen as parts of a room: "When
we had thoroughly examin'd this Head with all its Apartments,
and its several kinds of Furniture, we put up the Brain, such as it
was . . ." (*Spectator,* II, 573). The beau is imaginatively shown
to possess a pineal gland, the very seat of the soul, that

> smelt very strong of Essence and Orange-Flower Water, and
> was encompassed with a kind of Horny Substance, cut into a
> thousand little Faces or Mirrours, which were imperceptible to
> the naked Eye, insomuch that the Soul, if there had been any
> here, must have been always taken up in contemplating her
> own Beauties. (*Spectator,* II, 571)

The coquet receives no kinder treatment, for she possesses a heart
whose outer surface is "extremely slippery, and the *Mucro,* or
Point, so very cold withal, that upon endeavouring to take hold of
it, it glided through the Fingers like a smooth piece of Ice" (*Spectator,* II, 595). The subtle medical terminology gives the two
dream visions the pseudoscientific, nonsentimental, detached tone
that makes them succeed as social satire.

Two of Addison's best treatments of courtship and married life
are characteristically presented as imaginative tales—"The Modern Women of Hensberg" (No. 499) and "A Sale of London
Women" (No. 511). His method of handling the material in these
visions is through letters from Will Honeycomb, which gives the
visions a different tone from those narrated by the sedate Mr.
Spectator. The topics, scornful of women, furthermore are quite
appropriately placed in the hands of Will, who is an inveterate
failure with the fair sex. The humorous cynicism is believable
coming from his pen.

Will Honeycomb in "Modern Women of Hensburg" brings the

dream vision down from the misty plateau of abstract thought to the foothills of local life, but he does so with the same basic methods noted in the earlier allegories. The story is precipitated by a group discussion of the famous story of the women of Hensberg, who were allowed by the Duke of Bavaria to carry anything out of their besieged town that they could carry, and they carried their husbands. Will had asked the women in his group what they would have saved and upon going to bed fell into his dream. The dream gives him an opportunity to show what he thinks is the greatest concern of English women. Beginning with " 'I saw a Town of this Island, which shall be nameless' " (*Spectator*, IV, 270), one is never carried away from local England. In the language of Will Honeycomb, comments on Flanders lace, brocades, and Bolonia lapdogs add credibility to his narrative topic, as it instills variety into a story type that had been used for so long. Yet another reason Addison chose Honeycomb is concealed in Will's comments at the close of "A Sale of London Women" (No. 511):

> "I fancy thou wouldst like such a Vision, had I Time to finish it; because, to talk in thy own way, there is a Moral in it. Whatever thou may'st think of it, prithee do not make any of thy queer Apologies for this Letter, as thou didst for my last. The Women love a gay lively Fellow, and are never angry at the Railleries of one who is their known Admirer. . . ." (*Spectator*, IV, 316)

In these two dream visions, then, Addison fits the narrator to the nature of the subject matter—one of the essential gifts of a successful writer of fiction.

Three other moral dream visions, Budgell's "Love and Old Age" (No. 301), Steele's "A Vision of Mt. Parnassus" (No. 514), and "Heavenly and Worldly Wisdom" (No. 524), are presented also by correspondents, though unnamed, who relate their stories in letter form. Budgell's is particularly enhanced by this device since it concerns a dream a man writes in a letter to his cool beloved (not to Mr. Spectator). The audience for which it was written, represented by his beloved, would have been attracted by the vision of a beautiful woman repulsing Youth and Love only to be caught by old Age. Withholding information in this case is effective, as it was not for Mr. Spectator in No. 3 especially, for its vagueness of punishment is perhaps most suggestive of all to the female mind: " '. . . I will not Shock you with a Description of it: I was so startled at the Sight that my Sleep immediately left me, and I found my self awake, at leasure to consider of a Dream which seems too extraordinary to be without a Meaning . . .' " (*Spectator*, III, 78). Steele's dream vision again employs the pattern of the narrator's falling asleep while reading a classical volume (Virgil). The plot develops with the aid of the personified abstractions Solitude, Silence, and Contemplation. Steele's tendency to be more sentimental than Addison, however, can be noticed in such a line as " 'I was at once touch'd with Pleasure at my own Happiness, and Compassion at the Sight of their [people along the path of Virtue] inextricable Errors' " (*Spectator*, IV, 329). "Heavenly and Worldly Wisdom" likewise follows this pattern of handling the material, and the subject matter also evolves around the allegorical vision of the Spring of Self-Love, which forms the two streams of Heavenly Wisdom and Worldly Wisdom.[6]

Steele's "Transformation of Fidelio into a Looking-Glass" (No. 392) is interesting and noteworthy because of its method of narration, its episodic structure, and its nonawakening conclusion. In this piece Mr. Spectator does the dreaming, but the account is couched in the words of Fidelio, the personification of the mirror he looks into. Fidelio, the mirror, relates his ordeals with the women in his life, the last one of whom contacted smallpox and stabbed him to the heart. Although the action is described indirectly, the details are very carefully chosen, particularly regarding Narcissa, his murderess, in order to convey her mental anguish.

"However natural and formless the *short story* may sometimes

give the impression of being, however much it may appear to be
. . . the unadorned report of an action," comment the authors of
A Handbook of Literature, "a distinguishing characteristic of the
GENRE is that it is consciously *made,* that it reveals itself, upon
careful analysis, to be the result of conscious craftsmanship and
artistic skill."[7] That the dream vision-cum-allegory in the *Spectator* demonstrates, on the whole, such craftsmanship is evident
from the previous analysis and the survey of the subject matter,
the methods of handling the material, and the varied fictional
techniques in the seventeen examples. In No. 501 Mr. Spectator
reflected upon his use of the form, saying,

> As some of the finest Compositions among the Ancients are in
> Allegory, I have endeavoured, in several of my Papers, to re-
> vive that way of Writing, and hope I have not been altogether
> unsuccessful in it: For I find there is always a great Demand
> for those particular Papers. . . . (*Spectator,* IV, 275)

It was perhaps the great variety of techniques employed in a
single form that insured this demand. "Not altogether unsuccessful," Mr. Spectator's words, is a modest appraisal.

5

The Oriental Tale

There is a Story in the
Arabian Nights Tales, of . . .
—Mr. Spectator, *Spectator* No. 195

The Orient has always seemed to Western man to be something of an enigma. Unknown, it appeals to his curiosity. Exotic, it stirs up his longings for the strange, different, and unusual. Rich, it fulfills his desire for a Heaven on Earth. Ancient, it represents through its literature the knowledge that comes all too often only through bitter experience. Interest in the East was accelerated during the reign of Elizabeth by the characteristically Renaissance voyages of exploration, discovery, and commerce; and this unquenchable curiosity continued in the seventeenth century in the works of travelers, historians, translators of French heroic romances, dramatists, and Orientalists (in England the translations of the pseudo-oriental heroic romances of Mlle. de Scudéry and others became immensely popular, and Restoration plays were written on similar subjects). Sir Roger L'Estrange's version of *The Fables of Bidpai* (1692) and the appearance of *Turkish Tales* (1708) added to the influx of eastern material into England, material that gave the literate a vague acquaintance with the Orient. But it was, according to Martha Pike Conant, the "sudden advent of the *Arabian Nights,* full of the life, the colour, and the glamour of the East—even in the Gallicized version of Antoine Galland—[that] naturally opened a new chapter in the history of oriental fiction in England."[1] Galland, who brought the genie out of the bottle, popularized the tales in France, and a partial English translation of his French edition in 1706 widened the influence of his efforts in Great Britain.[2] The *Spectator*, not surprisingly, capitalized on this rejuvenated literary interest in the Orient and helped it "out of Closets and Libraries, Schools and Colleges, to dwell in Clubs and Assemblies, at Tea-Tables, and in Coffee-Houses."

The oriental tale and eastern material are not extensively employed in the *Spectator*, and, as with the fable, Addison is the author of all but one of the issues where such material occurs. Used selectively and in a number of ways and for several different reasons, however, the oriental tale adds variety to the short fiction related by Mr. Spectator and his correspondents. Melvin R. Watson rightly claims that "Addison's importance in the development of the oriental tale in England—and here again he is the dominant figure—lies not in what or how much he used but what he did with the material," since "*The Arabian Nights* and the various other collections of Persian and Oriental tales would have been popular and imitated had Addison never touched such material. . . ."[3] The aim here, therefore, is to present a clear and accurate description of the fifteen oriental-colored short stories and anecdotes scattered throughout the *Spectator*, with a view to determining what Addison, primarily, did with his material.

"By 'oriental,'" Conant says in her introduction, "I mean pertaining to or derived from 'those countries, collectively, that begin with Islam on the eastern Mediterranean and stretch through Asia,' with—so far as this specific treatment of the subject goes—one notable exception, Palestine."[4] Her definition is broad, permitting the inclusion of a broad spectrum of fictional material; for this reason it has been used as the guideline for the selection of stories and anecdotes included in this chapter. The fifteen stories or anecdotes of this classification include the following: Addison's "Observations by Four Indian Kings" (No. 50), "Mahomet's Journey to the Seven Heavens" (No. 94), "The Adventures of the Sultan of Egypt" (No. 94), "Sick King Cured by Exercise with Drugged Mallet" (No. 195), "Moses, God, Old Man, and Little Boy" (No. 237), "Dervise Who Mistakes Palace for Inn" (No. 289), "Pugg the Monkey" (No. 343), "Courageous Muly Moluc, Emperor of Morocco" (No. 349), "Persian Marriage-Auction" (No. 511), "Merchant Buying Old Woman in Sack" (No. 511), and Girolamo Gigli's "Letter from the Emperor of China to the Pope" (No. 545), and two fables and two dream visions previously discussed—"The Vision of Mirzah" (No. 159), "Fable of Drop of Water Which Became a Pearl" (No. 293), "Sultan Mahmoud and His Vizier" (No. 512) and "The Story of Alnaschar" (No. 535).[5] As previously mentioned, Mr. Spectator does not always keep the various types separate, a fact that is illustrated in "The Vision of Mirzah," where he blends dream vision, allegory, and oriental-eastern material into an imaginative original masterpiece.

The eleven remaining numbers fall naturally into three groups —moralistic, philosophic, and satiric. "The propensity to moralize and to philosophize, the love of satire, and the incipient romantic spirit,"[6] which Conant sees as a mark of the age, are everywhere evident in the selections. On the whole, the eleven numbers are mainly abridged or paraphrased from printed collections, but Addison presents them in a new context and makes alterations to fit his purposes. Some of them are illustrations, some are mere anecdotes to emphasize the point of a discussion, and some (the satirical ones) are presented in the form of letters. Addison's method of handling his material and the classification of the subject matter, in conjunction with how he used the tales, provide an interesting explanation of how the *Spectator* became a success with the public. Conant remarks that

> Even in the hands of Addison and Steele the oriental tale was speedily utilized to inculcate right living and was made into a story "with a purpose,"—in a word, became moralistic. The avowed aim of the *Spectator* and the *Tatler* was to reconcile wit and morality, to entertain and to preach, to hold the mirror of kindly ridicule up to society, to smile away the follies or

vices of the world, and to present serene, temperate, and beautiful ideals of thought and of conduct.[7]

The fiction that contains eastern material or is in fact an oriental story is permeated with this spirit.

The satirical oriental pieces—"Observations by Four Indian Kings" (No. 50), "Pugg the Monkey" (No. 343), and "Letter from the Emperor of China to the Pope" (No. 545)—all have one thing in common: they are related by a person other than Mr. Spectator and are presented in the form of an objective report or letter. Mr. Spectator merely does his editorial duty in presenting them to his readers; he avoids, therefore, any direct attack the satire might precipitate and continues his image as the friend to all. For example, in the "Observations by Four Indian Kings" Mr. Spectator goes out of his way to disassociate himself from the story that follows: "I have, since their Departure, employed a Friend to make many Enquiries of their Landlord the Upholsterer relating to their Manners and Conversation, as also concerning the Remarks which they made in this Country: For next to the forming a right Notion of such Strangers, I should be desirous of learning what Ideas they have conceived of us" (*Spectator*, I, 211–12).

In "Observations by Four Indian Kings" Addison employs a variation of the "discovered manuscript" method to present his material with a great degree of verisimilitude. Here Mr. Spectator is the editor, the interpreter, the presenter:

> The Upholsterer finding my Friend very inquisitive about these his Lodgers, brought him some time since a little Bundle of Papers, which he assured him were written by King *Sa Ga Yean Qua Rash Tow*, and, as he supposes, left behind by some Mistake. These Papers are now translated, and contain abundance of very odd Observations, which I find this little Fraternity of Kings made during their Stay in the Isle of *Great Britain*. I shall present my Reader with a short Specimen of them in this Paper, and may perhaps communicate more to him hereafter. In the Article of *London* are the following Words, which

without Doubt are meant of the Church of St. *Paul*. (*Spectator*,
I, 212)

The subject matter of this report by the Indian King concerns the
day-to-day life of London.

The purpose of the piece is to satirize London life—political,
religious, and social (both male and female)—in a lighthearted
but penetrating manner. The choice of the narrator is superb, for
he is one who is an objective, naive, ignorant foreigner who sees
things realistically. To him, and to his companions, the goings-on
are seen not from the force of habit, the expediencies of policy, or
the demands of fashion. The whirl of London, and the people who
produce it, are pictured as a fantastic network of shallow vestiges
of surface show. Addison employs a brilliant stroke of irony by
having Mr. Spectator comment, in conclusion, in a mock-serious
manner about the views of the Indian Kings:

> I cannot likewise forbear observing, That we are all guilty in
> some Measure of the same narrow Way of Thinking which we
> meet with in this Abstract of the *Indian* Journal; when we fancy
> the Customs, Dresses, and Manners of other Countries are
> ridiculous and extravagant, if they do not resemble those of our
> own. (*Spectator*, I, 215)

The Indian King's story has only a trace of oriental material—
just enough, as a matter of fact, to give it the desired tone and an
air of credibility. The Indian Kings, ironically, were *American*,
and the orientalisms are actually used to convey a sense of primi-
tive simplicity. The narrator could, in fact, be *any* foreign observer who is new to England, and his personality is enhanced
only incidentally by the eastern material or references to the romantic wilds of the world beyond. It is only in the semblance of
orientalism or primitivism that Addison is interested—that is, in
the *image* of the unknown or unfamiliar as instilled through allu-
sions and word choice. Whigs and Tories become rather vague
"Monsters": " 'Our other Interpreter used to talk very much of a

kind of Animal called a *Tory,* that was as great a Monster as a *Whig,* and would treat us as ill for being Foreigners.'" Speaking as any educated Englishman should (the translation is not literal), the Indian King continues: "'These two Creatures, it seems, are born with a secret Antipathy to one another, and engage when they meet as naturally as the Elephant and the Rhinoceros'" (*Spectator,* I, 213). The "Elephant and the Rhinoceros" reference puts enough of the aura of distant lands about the narrator to last until the narrator, using the same technique, casually mentions "those beautiful Feathers with which we adorn our Heads" in the next paragraph. This story by a foreign observer, a broadly satirical one, is clearly aimed at the improvement of the taste and habits of the reader; and in it the oriental material is, like the Indian Kings themselves, a speck of curious interest in otherwise thoroughly English surroundings.

The story of "Pugg the Monkey" (No. 343) satirizes the gullibility of women in general and illustrates the philosophic idea of the transmigration of souls in particular. Will Honeycomb relates the account of Jack Freelove's writing a letter and leaving it with his mistress's monkey, whom the lady assumes wrote it. In no sense is the anecdote more than an illustration of the idea of souls transmigrating after death, but it is enhanced by the touch of orientalism that is the monkey itself. Of course the idea of the transmigration of souls has been attributed to oriental philosophy also. The story is original with Addison.

The extent to which the authors of the *Spectator* went in order to give verisimilitude to their satiric oriental material is evidenced nowhere so well as in "Letter from the Emperor of China to the Pope" (No. 545), which was written by the Italian journalist Girolamo Gigli (See *Spectator,* IV, 449*n*). Indeed, both the Italian original and the English translation are printed in order to emphasize the authenticity of the letter from the giant of the Orient. The opening paragraph sets the tone of verisimilitude in its detailed eastern atmosphere, its romantic names, and its magnified use of figures:

"The Favourite Friend of GOD *Gionnata* the VIIth, most power-
ful above the most powerful of the Earth, highest above the
highest under the Sun and Moon, who sits on a Throne of
Emerald of *China,* above a 100 Steps of Gold, to interpret the
Language of GOD to the Faithful, and who gives Life and
Death to 115 Kingdoms, and 170 Islands; he writes with the
Quill of a Virgin *Ostrich,* and sends Health and Increase of old
Age." (*Spectator*, IV, 451)

But the most excellent touch of all is the style that enhances the
verisimilitude. The language is exotic, lush, florid, fitting in every
way the Englishman's idea of how an oriental king should write:

"Being arrived at the Time of our Age, in which the Flower
of our Royal Youth ought to ripen into Fruit towards old Age,
to comfort therewith the Desire of our devoted People, and to
propagate the Seed of that Plant which must protect them: We
have determined to accompany our selves with an high Amorous
Virgin, suckled at the Breast of a wild Lioness, and a meek
Lamb, and imagining with our selves that your *European* Roman
People is the Father of many unconquerable and chaste Ladies,
We stretch out our powerful Arm to embrace one of them, and
she shall be one of your Nieces, or the Niece of some other
great Latin Priest, the Darling of God's Right Eye." (*Spectator*,
IV, 451)

With such credibility as this—names, details, tone—the piece effectively directs a gentle satiric blow towards the exclusiveness of the
Catholics. In this number—the last in the original series with
oriental material—the technique of handling the material is not
much different from what was observed in "Observation by Four
Indian Kings" (No. 50), but the improvement in artistry is remarkable. Instead of ornamentation, the eastern material is integrated into the whole and is consistent with the character of the
storyteller.

Seven oriental tales occur as illustrations in philosophic or
moral expositions and do not appear strictly for their narrative
value, although Addison says on one occasion that the oriental

tale is "a Speculation that is more uncommon, and may therefore
perhaps be more entertaining" (*Spectator*, I, 398). In No. 94 Addison presents two stories, both of which illustrate the previous
discussion of Locke's and Malebranche's ideas about the subjectivity of time. The first, hardly more than an anecdote, recounts
Mahomet's journey to the Seven Heavens "in so small a Space of
Time, that *Mahomet*, at his Return, found his Bed still warm"
(*Spectator*, I, 400). The second illustration, "The Adventures of
of the Sultan of Egypt," is then neatly linked to this anecdote because it is the Sultan's disbelief in the incident of Mahomet's life
that precipitates his conflict with a great doctor of law (who then
proves it to him). The story is full of exotic fantasy: the Sultan
dips his head into a tub of water and finds himself at the foot of
a mountain on a seashore; he eventually marries, has seven sons
and seven daughters, is reduced to great want, and finally one
day before prayers "according to the Custom of the *Mahometans*"
he goes into the sea to bathe; he then appears back at his own tub
after his first plunge (*Spectator*, I, 400-01). Implicit in the tale
itself, Mr. Spectator's narrative voice makes the point of the illustration explicit:

> The *Mahometan* Doctor took this Occasion of instructing the
> Sultan, that nothing was impossible with God; and that *He*,
> with whom a Thousand Years are but as one Day, can if he
> pleases make a single Day, nay a single Moment, appear to
> any of his Creatures as a thousand Years.

That Mr. Spectator intends the oriental stories to be taken seriously as illustrations, rather than as the "entertainment" held out at
the beginning as an enticement, is then made plain: "I shall leave
my Reader to compare these Eastern Fables with the Notions of
those two great Philosophers whom I have quoted in this Paper
. . ." (*Spectator*, I, 401).

In No. 511 Addison again uses two stories related by Will
Honeycomb in a letter to the editor to illustrate his topic, which
is, ironically, that stories can be used very successfully as a means

of giving advice. Will Honeycomb is the perfect narrator because he is the kind of person who would logically tell incidents from other sources, claiming that they were first-hand experience. Once more, in the beginning the prospect of entertainment is held out to the reader, and at the same time Honeycomb places the stories into a definite place-time-situation context. As in much of the later fiction of the eighteenth and nineteenth centuries, there is the old storyteller or narrator talking directly to his audience:

> " . . . I have lately met with two pure Stories for a *Spectator,* which I am sure will please mightily, if they pass through thy Hands. The first of them I found by chance in an *English* book called *Herodotus,* that lay in my Friend *Dapperwit's* Window, as I visited him one Morning. It luckily opened in the Place where I met with the following Account." (*Spectator,* IV, 314)

The first story, "Persian Marriage Auction," relates how public money was given to the ugly women in that country so that they would be attractive to men. The second, "The Merchant Who Purchased an Old Woman in a Sack," illustrates the philosophic idea of good fortune, because "she proved an excellent Wife, and procured him all the Riches from her Brother that she had promised him" (*Spectator,* IV, 316).

"The Dervise Who Mistakes a Palace for an Inn" (No. 289) is used in a similar manner to exemplify Mr. Spectator's ideas on death, which are expressed at the beginning of the essay: "how can we, without supposing our selves under the constant Care of a Supreme Being, give any possible Account for that nice proportion which we find in every great City, between the Deaths and Births of its Inhabitants, and between the number of Males, and that of Females, who are brought into the world?" (*Spectator,* III, 27). Mr. Spectator then says that he will relate a story "which I have some where read in the Travels of Sir *John Chardin*" to illustrate his point about the perpetual renewal of life in the world. The story is typical of the oriental material in the *Spectator* in that names and outward appearances of the piece are eastern while the situation itself is universal. The use of reported dialogue, however, gives immediacy to character interaction, which is the basis of the conflict. A dervise mistakes a king's palace for a caravansary and is questioned about this audacity by the king, to whom the dervise turns:

> Sir, says the *Dervise*, give me leave to ask your Majesty a Question or two. Who were the Persons that lodged in this House when it was first Built? the King replied, *His Ancestors.* And who, says the *Dervise*, was the last Person that lodged here? The King replied, *His Father.* And who is it, says the *Dervise*, that lodges here at present? the King told him *that it was he himself.* And who, says the Dervise will be here after you? The King answer'd, *The young Prince his Son.* "Ah, Sir, said the *Dervise*, a House that changes its Inhabitants so often, and receives such a perpetual Succession of Guests, is not a Palace but a *Caravansary.*" (*Spectator*, III, 30–31)

The climax is admirable. Here is certainly the effect of orientalism, but it is not pervasive in the story; by substituting "inn" for "Caravansary" and "peddler" for "Dervise" Addison could have created a totally different effect. But it probably would have lost much of its appeal and power as an illustration to his readers.

In No. 237 Addison employs an oriental tale, "Moses, God, Old Man, and Little Boy" (from Jewish tradition), to illustrate the fact that man cannot judge God's acts with reason and that God acts with justice at all times. The structure of the story is quite similar to "The Vision of Mirzah"; in this case God and Moses on a mountain top contemplate the world below:

> At the Foot of the Mountain there issued out a clear Spring of Water, at which a Soldier alighted from his Horse to Drink. He was no sooner gone than a little Boy came to the same Place, and finding a Purse of Gold which the Soldier had dropped, took it up and went away with it. Immediately after this came an Infirm old Man, weary with Age and Travelling, and having quenched his Thirst, sat down to rest himself by the side of the Spring. The Soldier missing his Purse returns to search for

it, and demands it of the old Man, who affirms he had not seen it, and appeals to Heaven in witness of his Innocence. The Soldier, not believing his Protestations, kills him. *Moses* fell on his face with Horror and Amazement, when the Divine Voice thus prevented his Expostulation, "Be not surprised, *Moses,* nor ask why the Judge of the whole Earth has suffer'd this thing to come to pass; the Child is the Occasion that the Blood of the old Man is spilt; but know, that the old Man whom thou sawest was the Murderer of that Child's Father." (*Spectator,* II, 423)[8]

This story has the beautiful simplicity of the Scriptures; its structure reinforces the climax by making the reader sympathize with Moses' viewpoint. As an illustration of divine justice it is excellent.

Such employment of the oriental tale to emphasize a moral or philosophic idea is seen also in No. 349, where Addison relates a story by the Abbot of Vertot.[9] The story is of Muly Moluc, Emperor of Morocco, who refuses to permit his soldiers to learn of his death so that they can continue to fight on to victory on the battlefield. Again, this illustrates courage clearly, but the episode has a universality that transcends its oriental flavor, which in Addison's account is mainly a result of the precise use of eastern names.

On one occasion Mr. Spectator uses oriental material not to illustrate a moral or philosophic idea but to introduce his thoughts on the value of exercise. "The Sick King Cured by Exercise with Drugged Mallet" (No. 195), from the *Arabian Nights,* is a mere anecdote that Addison knew would appeal to his readers. In this number Mr. Spectator assumes his accustomed role of the personal storyteller chatting with his audience. He begins, "There is a Story in the *Arabian Nights Tales,* of a King who had long languished under an ill Habit of Body, and had taken abundance of Remedies to no purpose" (*Spectator,* II, 263). Not until the strange tale is told does he suggest to the reader that it does indeed "shew us how beneficial Bodily Labour is to Health, and that Exercise is the most effectual Physick" (*Spectator,* II, 263).

Although Addison did not write much original oriental fiction

in the *Spectator* and although in some of the tales discussed there
is only the slightest eastern coloring, what he did with the material is interesting to the student of eighteenth-century literature.
In several numbers he employs the form, presented as a report
or letter from an objective observer, as a vehicle for his satire on
English politics, religion, and society. But, in addition, Addison
gives the oriental and pseudo-oriental material an illustrative
function and a moralistic, philosophic direction that it maintained
in English periodicals throughout the century.[10] As Melvin Watson says,

> Addison's influence on the oriental tale throughout the rest of
> the century (and it was admittedly great) was achieved by his
> casual use of oriental material as illustrations for some half-
> dozen of his moral discussions. His imitators either wrote moral
> oriental stories or added moral touches to existing material.
> Actually Addison, except once, had done neither; he had simply
> planted a few of the stories in his garden of morality.[11]

The morality, like the philosophy (except in No. 343), is not
characteristically oriental in the stories, and Martha Pike Conant
cogently observes that the industry and economy, health and
cleanliness, prudence and justice, the act of giving advice and
seeking instruction are in the final analysis "the Addisonian code
of virtues in oriental guise."[12] This is true. But as pieces of short
fiction they are significant because they offer—however fantastic,
however weak in characterization, however brilliant in setting,
however unoriginal as a group—one asset that some of the other
forms in the *Spectator* lack, that is, the element of plot. The series
of accounts about Sir Roger de Coverley in the country, making
up an accumulative episode, possess admirable characterization
and a well-defined background, but the absence of plot alone de-
nies to the paper full credentials as a novel. The plot of the oriental tales, on the other hand, is normally strong in incident, and
there is a movement of action developing toward a conscious
climax.[13] A series of incidents that are integrally linked with each

other focus the reader's attention on the working out of a situation (a conflict). This element of connected actions emphasizes the importance of plot, in conjunction with characterization and background, in short fiction. The oriental tales in the *Spectator* provide such emphasis.

6

Miscellaneous Forms

We are, indeed, so often conversant with one Sett of Objects, and tired out with so many repeated Shows of the same Things, that whatever is *new* or *uncommon* contributes a little to vary Human Life, and to divert our Minds, for a while, with the Strangeness of its Appearance: It serves us for a kind of Refreshment, and takes off from that Satiety we are apt to complain of in our usual and ordinary Entertainments.

—Mr. Spectator, *Spectator* No. 412

In order to vary his material and to present it in as many refreshing ways as possible, Mr. Spectator sometimes used story types that were "*new* or *uncommon*" because of their infrequent appearance in his periodical or because of their particular treatment or selected use in the *Spectator*. Such forms include the mock-sentimental tale, the fabliau and rogue literature, the satirical adventure story, the domestic apologue, and the exemplum. Each of the miscellaneous forms added to the appeal of the *Spectator* since the reader could never anticipate exactly in which direction any given issue was to turn.

THE MOCK-SENTIMENTAL TALE

The *Spectator* published one mock-sentimental tale,[1] and somewhat surprisingly Richard Steele, the author of *The Conscious Lovers*, was the one who wrote it. Overindulgence in sentimentalism, however, had been an object of satire in the *Spectator*. In

No. 44 Addison satirized the pathetic effects of increasing the number of suffering children on the stage:

> And as I am inform'd, a young Gentleman who is fully determin'd to break the most obdurate Hearts, has a Tragedy by him, where the first Person that appears upon the Stage, is an afflicted Widow in her Mourning-Weeds, with half a Dozen fatherless Children attending her, like those that usually hang about the Figure of Charity. Thus several Incidents that are beautiful in a good Writer, become ridiculous by falling into the Hands of a bad one. (*Spectator*, I, 187)

Also in Steele's *Tatler* Nos. 50–51 Addison had satirized the sentimental "Histories" of love and gallantry then enjoying a vogue in polite circles; "The History of Orlando the Fair" is a running parody of novels like the celebrated *Portugese Letters* (1678) and Mrs. Behn's *Philander and Sylvia* (1683).[2] That Steele also saw the possibilities of parodying such sentimental fiction and drama, especially in 1711 when it was viewed with less favor by the "good writers," is only natural. At any rate, his mock-sentimental tale "Sir Roger and the Widow" (No. 113) illustrates his imaginative powers in short fiction and particularly his appealing techniques of narration.

The sentimentalism that Steele satirizes in "Sir Roger and the Widow" involves those emotions emphasized most by the writers of the time: pleasant feelings of complacency, contentment, relief, and repose; painful feelings of sadness, sorrow, grief, and regret; and mixed feelings of sympathy and pity.[3] It is the sentimentalism defined by Ernest A. Baker as "that unbalanced state of mind which revels in emotion, especially grief and compassion, and decides its moral problems according to the reactions of feeling."[4] Although Steele's tale deals with a tragedy of love rather than with a tragedy of death, it effectively assails this kind of overindulgence in sentiment, "especially the conscious effort to induce emotion in order to analyze or enjoy it," and, "also the failure to restrain or evaluate emotion through the exercise of the judgment."[5] An analysis of the mock-sentimental tale reveals the artistry of the author.

"Sir Roger and the Widow" is a frame story. It is related by Sir Roger de Coverley and directed toward a specific audience—Mr. Spectator—in a personal, informal style. The headlink, much in the manner of Chaucer's *Canterbury Tales,* gives the reader an idea of the character's present state of mind or attitude toward the story, which he then tells. The two men, Sir Roger and Mr. Spectator, in their conversation smoothly glide into an introduction of the story itself:

> It happened this Evening, that we fell into a very pleasing Walk at a distance from his House; as soon as we came into it, "It is, quoth the good Old Man, looking around him with a Smile, very hard that any part of my Land should be settled upon one who has used me so ill as the perverse Widow did, and yet I am sure I could not see a Sprig of any Bough of this whole Walk of Trees, but I should reflect upon her and her Severity. . . . " (*Spectator,* I, 463)

After Sir Roger spills out his account of the affair with the perverse widow to Mr. Spectator, we return again to the frame in which Mr. Spectator guides the reaction of *his* audience to the emotional outpouring of the old man. It is the attitude of Mr. Spectator that seals with irony, humor, and exaggeration the mockery of sensibility Sir Roger demonstrates.

The tone of quiet pleasure with which Mr. Spectator points out Sir Roger's complete captivation by his widow—accomplished through straight-faced overstatement and exaggeration—is made evident even in the motto at the beginning:

> His Words, his Looks imprinted in her Heart,
> Improve the Passion, and increase the Smart.
> —Virgil, *Aeneid,* 4.4 (Dryden)

And especially interesting is Mr. Spectator's subtle reaction to Sir Roger's opening panegyric of the woman. Repeating praise after praise with his hurting heart, Sir Roger sentimentalizes,

"She has certainly the finest Hand of any Woman in the World. You are to know this was the Place wherein I used to muse upon her, and by that Custom I can never come into it, but the same tender Sentiments revive in my Mind, as if I had actually walked with that Beautiful Creature under these Shades. I have been Fool enough to Carve her Name on the Bark of several of these Trees, so unhappy is the Condition of Men in Love to attempt the removing of their Passion by the Methods which serve only to imprint it deeper. She has certainly the finest Hand of any Woman in the World." (*Spectator*, I, 463)

Mr. Spectator notes with a little more than his normal taciturnity that "Here followed a profound Silence." After the long pause, Sir Roger, it is reported, entered upon his account "of this great Circumstance in his Life," which gave Mr. Spectator a clear picture of the cheerful man before he "received that Stroke which has ever since affected his Words and Actions" (*Spectator*, I, 463–64). But the reader suspects, and should know, that Mr. Spectator actually views the circumstances as anything but "great" and the "Stroke" as anything but severe.

That Mr. Spectator is the vehicle by which Steele emphasizes the ludicrousness of Sir Roger's sentimental story is reinforced by the same tone of controlled humor at the conclusion. Ironically, Sir Roger (who thinks he is in complete control of his emotions) has not allowed reason to guide his reactions. He begins to "rave" about the widow, Mr. Spectator says, "tho' he has so much Command of himself, as not directly to mention her. . . ." Finally, the paper is concluded with an epigram that leaves not the least doubt about the attitude of Mr. Spectator. This epigram humorously depicts his friend's condition:

Let Rufus *weep, rejoice, stand, sit, or walk,*
Still he can nothing but of Naevia *talk:*
Let him eat, drink, ask Questions, *or dispute,*
Still he must speak *of* Naevia, or be mute.
He writ to his Father, ending with this Line,
I am, my Lovely Naevia, ever thine. (*Spectator*, I, 467)

Thus Mr. Spectator reacts to the commentary of Sir Roger throughout the story and in so doing forces a reaction not of sympathy and pity for Sir Roger but of humor and delight and amusement at the content and manner of his sentimental account, which induces emotion in order to enjoy it.

The subject matter of Sir Roger's story itself follows the normal course of most romantic fiction in that it deals with the course of romantic love, has a "humble" and "royal" character, and incorporates a "warlike" adventure. And as Orlando was "the universal flame of all the fair sex" in *Tatler* Nos. 50–51, so Sir Roger is " 'pretty tall, ride[s] well, and [is] very well Dressed, at the Head of a whole County' " with a feather in his hat and a horse well bitted (*Spectator*, I, 464). He is, in short, a caricature. The warlike adventure turns out to be, in part, Sheriff Roger de Coverley's encounter with the Widow in court; actually it was never much of a contest, for Sir Roger says that she no sooner cast her bewitching eyes on him but " 'I bowed like a great surprized Booby, and knowing her Cause to be the first which came on, I cry'd like a Captivated Calf as I was . . .' " (*Spectator*, I, 464). The episodic plot (another characteristic of sentimental prose tales) then turns to Sir Roger's meeting with the Widow at her home, a battle of wits where the tongue replaces the sword, an encounter that momentarily fills him " 'with such an Awe as made [him] Speechless' " (*Spectator*, I, 465). Her conversation was to Sir Roger indeed " 'as Learned as the best Philosopher in *Europe* could possibly make' " (*Spectator*, I, 466). Placing such words in the mouth of Sir Roger is a hilarious performance of gentle, mocking wit.

Aside from the episodic plot, the method Sir Roger uses in telling his story to Mr. Spectator reflects the methods of the sentimental tales. There is a self-analysis of the psychological state of the despairing lover (again exaggerated and overstated), which is heavy with irony:

> "I can assure you, Sir, were you to behold her, you would be in the same Condition; for as her Speech is Musick, her Form

is Angelick; but I find I grow irregular while I am talking of her, but indeed it would be Stupidity to be unconcerned at such Perfection. Oh the Excellent Creature, she is as inimitable to all Women, as she is inaccessible to all Men—" (*Spectator*, I, 466)

There are, furthermore, set passages and speeches ("She has certainly the finest Hand of any Woman in the World" is repeated three times) and interspersed didactic material. Lastly, Sir Roger records his actual observations—observations that in sentimental fiction often brought tears to numerous eyes—that parody the popular fashion:

> "After she had done speaking to me, she put her Hand to her Bosom, and adjusted her Tucker. Then she cast her Eyes a little down, upon my beholding her too earnestly. They say she sings excellently, her Voice in her ordinary Speech has something in it inexpressibly sweet. You must know I dined with her at a publick Table the Day after I first saw her, and she helped me to some Tansy in the Eye of all the Gentlemen in the Country. . . . " (*Spectator*, I, 466)[6]

The effect of the story "Sir Roger and the Widow" comes primarily from the reader's recognition of the irony of Sir Roger's statements, and the amusement is derived through his trying to convince Mr. Spectator that he is justified in his emotions. Mr. Spectator, however, is not convinced, though Sir Roger thinks he is entirely sympathetic. And the audience knows that the story is not an example of genuine sentiment; Mr. Spectator (and behind him Steele) is too artistic in the techniques employed to enhance the mock sentiment of the episode. "Sir Roger and the Widow" is an imaginative excursion into the realm of the mock-sentimental tale: "It serves us for a kind of Refreshment, and takes off from that Satiety we are apt to complain of in our usual and ordinary Entertainments" (*Spectator*, III, 541). More refreshment of this quality would have been welcome in the *Spectator*.

THE FABLIAU AND ROGUE LITERATURE

The fabliau often has an ostensible moral appended to it, but it differs from the fable in that it normally does not have a serious purpose, always has human beings as characters, and maintains a realistic tone and manner.[7] The form need not be bawdy, however much this characteristic may be attached to it in the popular mind. More often than not fabliaux are comic, frankly coarse, and pervasively cynical in tone, especially in the treatment of women and in relation to actions between the sexes. They often contain tricks played by one person on another.[8] Addison's "The Male Mummy" (No. 90) is an example in the *Spectator*. Rogue literature, in the picaresque tradition, has some of the same characteristics but is clearly a different kind of fiction. If rogue literature may be defined as realistic but often comically absurd (prose) tales with a pervasively cynical attitude toward women, then the *Spectator* also has some half-dozen stories that conveniently fall into this category of short fiction. These include Steele's "Brunetta and Phillis" (No. 80), Addison's "Eginhart and Imma" (No. 181), Addison's "The Castilian and His Wife" (No. 198), Hughes's "Amanda" (No. 375), Steele's "Soldier and Country Girl" (No. 342), and Steele's "Sapphira and Rhynsault" (No. 491).

Spectator No. 90 concerns, at the outset, the Platonic conception of Hell, but near the end Mr. Spectator comments, "That I may a little alleviate the Severity of this my Speculation (which otherwise may lose me several of my polite Readers) I shall translate a Story that has been quoted upon another Occasion by one of the most learned Men of the present Age, as I find it in the Original" (*Spectator*, I, 382).[9] The story, "The Male Mummy," is a delightful fabliau. It admirably contrasts in tone with the opening high seriousness. It is comic, realistic, and absurd—all this so very entertaining and appealing in tone to the polite reader—and at the same time the story is unified with the structure of the essay: it is "a lively Representation of a Person lying under the Torments of such a Kind of Tantalism, or *Platonick* Hell, as that which we have now under Consideration" (*Spectator*, I, 382). The story is a double-edged sword.

"The Male Mummy" is a first-person narrative, related by Monsieur Pontignan, of a love adventure while he is in the country. It has the unity of mood, limited action, the limited number of characters, and a thematic significance that carries it beyond the triviality of its details of situation and circumstance. As in most fabliaux, the biter-bit motif is predominant. The rising action involves Pontignan's wooing of two ladies simultaneously, ladies who one day ask to wrap him up like a mummy in order to play a trick on someone else. The climax is fittingly humorous:

> "As I stood bolt upright upon one End in this antique Figure, one of the Ladies burst out a Laughing, 'And now *Pontignan,* says she, we intend to perform the Promise that we find you have extorted from each of us. You have often asked the Favour of us, and I dare say you are a better bred Cavalier than to refuse to go to Bed to Ladies that desire it of you.' " (*Spectator,* I, 383)

And the denouement is kept alive by the frank, realistic account by Pontignan of his reactions in this ridiculous situation:

> "You may easily guess at the Condition of a Man that saw a couple of the most beautiful Women in the World undrest and abed with him, without being able to stir Hand or Foot. I begged them to release me, and struggled all I could to get loose, which I did with so much Violence, that about Midnight they both leaped out of the Bed crying out they were undone: But seeing me safe they took their Posts again, and renewed their Raillery. Finding all my Prayers and Endeavours were lost, I compos'd my self as well as I could; and told them, that if they would not unbind me, I would fall asleep between them, and by that Means disgrace them for ever: But alas! this was impossible; could I have been disposed to it, they would have prevented me by several little ill-natured Caresses and Endearments which they bestow'd upon me. As much devoted as I am to Womankind, I would not pass such another Night to be Master of the Whole Sex." (*Spectator,* I, 383–84)

The cynicism lying at the base of the story, the imagistic view of a Platonic Hell, the comic absurdity, even the bawdiness are unified into an organic whole, economically told and altered to fit the purposes of the *Spectator*. Once again, in "The Male Mummy" Addison sets forth an old form in new wrappings.

In No. 80 Steele also wrote a story that employs the biter-bit motif of Addison's No. 90. This tale of "Brunetta and Phillis" is a humorously satirical look at two female rivals for attention in the world of fashion. The rivalry culminates in Phillis' buying a beautiful gown to show up Brunetta, who has meanwhile bought a copy for her maid, a situation that humiliates Phillis so much that she flees to Plymouth. The roguish behavior on the part of a delicate female is comically absurd and is in the tradition of the cynical, devilish, painful tricks of fabliaux.

The rising action, climax, and denouement of "Brunetta and Phillis" are presented with vivid description, details, and an excellent portrayal of character conflict. Also, one is able to detect and experience the "Anguish of Mind" of both the antagonist and protagonist. Steele creates characters here who are more than cardboard. But perhaps the fictional techniques of economy in short fiction—giving enough information but not too much—are the most outstanding features of this story (which is, incidentally, not presented as an illustration, for it begins the essay). In the first paragraph Steele masterfully sets the scene, introduces the characters, suggests the conflict and the controlling theme, reveals antecedent action, notes the time, and renders the situation comprehensible:

> In the year 1688, and on the same Day of that Year, were born in *Cheapside, London,* two Females of exquisite Feature and Shape; the one we shall call *Brunetta,* the other *Phillis.* A close Intimacy between their Parents made each of them the first Acquaintance the other knew in the World: They play'd, dressed Babies, acted Visitings, learned to Dance and make Curtesies, together. They were inseparable Companions in all the little Entertainments their tender Years were capable of: which innocent Happiness continued till the Beginning of their fifteenth Year, when it happened that Mrs. *Phillis* had an Head-dress

on which became her so very well, that instead of being be-
held any more with Pleasure for their Amity to each other,
the Eyes of the Neighbourhood were turned to remark them with
Comparison of their Beauty. They now no longer enjoyed the
Ease of Mind and pleasing Indolence in which they were formerly happy, but all their Words and Actions were misinter-
preted by each other, and every Excellence in their Speech and
Behaviour was looked upon as an Act of Emulation to surpass
the other. These Beginnings of Disinclination soon improved into
a Formality of Behaviour, a general Coldness, and by natural
Steps into an irreconcileable Hatred. (*Spectator,* I, 342–43)

Such an introduction is the work of a polished, conscious, and
effective raconteur.

In *Spectator* No. 181 Addison varies the approach and relates
the story of "Eginhart and Imma" to illustrate the fact that no
hardness of heart is so inexcusable as that of parents toward their
children. The story is quite sentimental, and it admirably shows
how Addison could employ the rogue-figure for moral purposes.
Eginhart, a noble member of a court and a rogue, goes to Prin-
cess Imma's apartments one night, and in the morning the new
fallen snow on the ground outside forces Imma to carry him
away so that the Emperor will not notice his tracks. This trick is
observed, however, and in the course of events the Emperor compassionately merely forces the man to marry his daughter "with a
Dower suitable to her Quality" (*Spectator,* II, 216).[10] Steele follows this rogue story with another in No. 182, but he varies the
technique of presentation and the tone of the story. "Alice Treadneedle's Maid" (No. 182) is conveyed in a letter from Alice, and
in details that are frank and humorous she writes about the time a
man tried to seduce her maid. With righteous indignation Alice
demands of Mr. Spectator:

> "In a Word, Sir, it is in the Power of you, and such as I hope
> you are, to make it as infamous to rob a poor Creature of her
> Honour as her Cloaths. I leave this to your Consideration, only
> take Leave, (which I cannot do without sighing) to remark to

you, that if this had been the Sense of Mankind thirty Years
ago, I should have avoided a Life spent in Poverty and Shame."
(*Spectator*, II, 218)

The name "Alice Treadneedle" and her exaggerated, serious tone
establish the satirical bent of the piece, which was probably presented mainly for amusement.

Perhaps the best example of rogue literature in the *Spectator* is
Addison's "The Castilian and His Wife" (No. 198), a story that
Mr. Spectator "lately heard from one of our *Spanish* Officers"
(*Spectator*, II, 277).[11] Addison combines a lusty story with the
sentimentalism that might appeal to his polite feminine audience.
The story is particularly strong in plot, which is episodic; things
happen quickly:

> The *Castilian* having made his Addresses to her and married
> her, they lived together in perfect Happiness for some Time;
> when at length the Husband's Affairs made it necessary for him
> to take a Voyage to the Kingdom of *Naples*, where a great Part
> of his Estate lay. The Wife loved him too tenderly to be left
> behind him. They had not been a Shipboard above a Day,
> when they unluckily fell into the Hands of an *Algerine* Pyrate,
> who carried the whole Company on Shore, and made them
> Slaves. The *Castilian* and his Wife had the Comfort to be under
> the same Master; who seeing how dearly they loved one an-
> other, and gasped after their Liberty, demanded a most exor-
> bitant Price for their Ransom. (*Spectator*, II, 277)

This opening section of love and physical imprisonment and trust
is then contrasted with the closing mood of hatred and spiritual
disenchantment and perfidy, and the rogue Renegado (who makes
it possible for the Castilian to go back for the ransom) is the
agent of cohesion between the two parts.

> The Renegado, during the Husband's Absence, so insinuated
> himself into the good Graces of his young Wife, and so turned
> her Head with Stories of Gallantry, that she quickly thought him
> the finest Gentleman she had ever conversed with. To be brief,

her Mind was quite alienated from the honest *Castilian,* whom she was taught to look upon as a formal old Fellow unworthy the Possession of so charming a Creature. She had been instructed by the Renegado how to manage herself upon his Arrival; so that she received him with an Appearance of the utmost Love and Gratitude, and at length perswaded him to trust their common Friend the Renegado with the Money he had brought over for their Ransome. . . . (*Spectator,* II, 278)

At this point the narrator, Mr. Spectator, shows his hand and by commenting guides the reader's reaction and also gives the story a personal touch:

I wish I could conceal the Sequel of this Story, but since I cannot I shall dispatch it in as few Words as possible. The *Castilian* having slept longer than ordinary the next Morning, upon his awaking found his Wife had left him: He immediately rose and enquired after her, but was told that she was seen with the Renegado about Break of Day. In a Word, her Lover having got all things ready for their Departure, they soon made their Escape out of the Territories of *Algiers,* carried away the Money, and left the *Castilian* in Captivity; who partly through the cruel Treatment of the incensed *Algerine* his Master, and partly through the unkind Usage of his unfaithful Wife, died some few Months after. (*Spectator,* II, 279)

No other rogue literature in the *Spectator* treats women so viciously and with such powerful cynicism. The sentiment is deftly handled, too, for Addison for the most part allows the action to speak for itself.[12]

The *Spectator*'s use of the fabliau and rogue literature represents, first of all, an effort to "alleviate the Severity" of Mr. Spectator's daily speculations, but however entertaining, absurd, and frivolous the tales may appear on the surface, the editors succeed in blending them with their avowed purpose of enlivening morality with wit. Two matters are most noteworthy about these categories of short fiction. Firstly, the material again is handled in a variety of ways—sometimes the story is told first and then the application is made, again the story comes on occasion as an illustration, and sometimes the tale is narrated by a letter writer who is a first-person participant. Secondly, an element lacking in a number of the Characters and sketches, plot, is here plentiful enough, and there is an even balance of realism on the one hand and sentimentalism on the other. What the stories lack in character portrayal is overbalanced by a generally unified thematic control, a sustained mood that fits each particular plot and situation, and vivid descriptions of characters engaged in unusual sexual activities.

THE SATIRICAL ADVENTURE STORY

The satirical adventure story belongs to a somewhat similar class of short fiction as the fabliau and rogue literature; it too is often comically absurd in its attempt to ridicule human vices and follies from an odd or rather impersonal point of view—usually by the imaginary experiences of some inanimate object. Steele's "The Adventures of a Shilling" in *Tatler* No. 249, in which a shilling gives an account of its life and adventures, is an example of this type of story that gives an entertaining image of human levity and cupidity. "Such stories were introduced quite casually in the *Tatler*," Robert D. Mayo points out, "but they were to have a very numerous progeny in later essay-serials and miscellanies in the form of the satirical or sentimental adventures of wigs, banknotes, pens, pocket handkerchiefs, and quires of paper. The writers of such stories, of course, were partly inspired by the popularity of novels like Coventry's *Pompey the Little* (1751), Mrs. Haywood's *Invisible Spy* (1755), and Johnstone's *Chrysal* (1760-1765), but it is important to remember that in the periodicals there was a much-older tradition for satirical adventure stories, dating back at least to 1710."[13] Part of the "numerous progeny in later essay-serials and miscellanies" that Mayo speaks of may be found in the *Spectator*, which contains two satirical adventure narratives.[14]

The best example of the satirical adventure narrative in the

Spectator is also a dream vision-cum-allegory—as might be expected from the form's characteristic picturing of human levity and cupidity. The narrative is "The Transformation of Fidelio into a Looking-Glass" (No. 392), which was analyzed in Chapter 4.[15] As then observed, the looking glass is given human characteristics and narrates his adventures with various women over a period of years. Each episode is fraught with satire on the frivolity and shallowness of women who are obsessed with appearance only. The choice of the looking glass to satirize people who mistake appearance for reality was a stroke of genius on Steele's part. The reader can never forget the irony that the mirror, the Shrine of Appearance, is nevertheless destroyed for its allegiance to the Temple of Truth. The use of the satirical adventure story in league with the dream vision and allegory is a remarkable fusion of story types into an imaginative narrative.

One other brief example of the satirical adventure narrative is is "The Masque" (No. 385), which is hardly more than an anecdote. It is not a series of adventures, but it is a single incident that highlights the cupidity of women. In the episode, which takes place one day as Sir Roger enters Spring-Garden, it is quite clear that the personified inanimate object is a metaphor for a certain type of woman. Yet the vignette is in the tradition of the satirical adventure story:

> He here fetched a deep Sigh, and was falling into a fit of musing, when a Masque, who came behind him, gave him a gentle Tap upon the Shoulder, and asked him if he would drink a Bottle of Mead with her? But the Knight being startled at so unexpected a Familiarity, and displeased to be interrupted in his Thoughts of the Widow, told her *She was a wanton Baggage,* and bid her go about her Business. (*Spectator,* III, 438)

This is by no means a developed story, but Steele does work the Masque into the narrative framework as a personified object for satirical reasons.

Thus, the satirical adventure story was not a popular form in the *Spectator*. Addison used it not at all, and Steele only twice. In No. 392 he succeeded admirably in creating a well-rounded narrative, one that provides a better understanding of how he approached the task of creating a short story out of the various possible forms available to him.

THE DOMESTIC APOLOGUE

The *Spectator*'s statement of policy set forth in No. 10 included, among other things, this comment: "I would therefore in a very particular Manner recommend these my Speculations to all well regulated Families, that set apart an Hour in every Morning for Tea and Bread and Butter; and would earnestly advise them for their Good to order this Paper to be punctually served up, and to be looked upon as a Part of the Tea Equipage" (*Spectator*, I, 44–45). Of course any number of the story types previously discussed could well serve as the bill of fare for such a familial gathering (all the narratives are more or less didactic), but perhaps the domestic apologues in the *Spectator* were intended to be the usual favorites for family consumption. Intermixed with the narratives of genteel society, visionary worlds, exotic lands, and high life are little domestic tragedies and tragicomedies of a sentimental turn that convey a useful lesson.

The domestic apologues in the *Spectator* always present people within the home and family. Many of them are also love stories, in which Steele (primarily) attacks the inhumanity of man, the harshness of parents, buying and selling in marriage, and the evils of jointures and settlements. The stories expound the advantages of mutual love and trust, unselfishness, and prudence among the middle and upper middle classes. According to Robert Mayo, in the *Tatler* some of "Steele's domestic tales are purely sentimental; in others irony and humor, satire and pathos, are blended in equal parts."[16] Mayo's overview is applicable as well to the tales of this variety in the *Tatler*'s direct descendant. Numerous references to domestic situations for illustrative purposes

occur, some of which approach the level of the narrative anec-
dote, but the most fully developed narrative domestic apologues
in the *Spectator* are Steele's "Laetitia and Daphne" (No. 33),
Steele's "Honoria and Flavia" (No. 91), Addison's "Eudoxus and
Leontine" (No. 123), Addison's "A Country Couple" (No. 128),
Addison's "The Gypsy Boy" (No. 130), Addison's "Constantia and
Theodosius" (No. 164), Addison's "Mariamne and Herod" (No.
171), Addison's "The Barbados Negroes" (No. 215), Steele's
"Father and Son" (No. 426), and "Cephalus and Procris" (No.
527)—a total of ten.[17]

In Steele's "Laetitia and Daphne" (No. 33), a domestic apologue that is related without an essayistic introduction, irony, humor, and satire are employed together. The purpose of the narrative is to satirize pretentiousness through ridicule, and Steele
wastes no time, after the main characters are mentioned, in setting
forth the controlling theme of his tale:

> A Friend of mine has two Daughters, whom I will call *Laetitia*
> and *Daphne;* The Former is one of the Greatest Beauties of the
> Age in which she lives, the Latter no way remarkable for any
> Charms in her Person. Upon this one Circumstance of their
> Outward Form, the Good and Ill of their Life seems to turn.
> (*Spectator*, I, 137)

Although the assertion that the two girls are daughters of "A
Friend of Mine" is intended to increase the credibility of the
story and to heighten the realism, the two are not individuals but
types that convey the universality of the satire. The two women,
indeed, are representations of dual forms of behavior, presented
in a style as balanced as they are:

> . . . *Laetitia* is as insipid a Companion, as *Daphne* is an agree-
> able one. *Laetitia*, confident of Favour, has studied no Arts to
> please; *Daphne*, despairing of any Inclination towards her Per-
> son, has depended only on her Merit. *Laetitia* has always some-
> thing in her Air that is sullen, grave and disconsolate. *Daphne*

has a Countenance that appears chearful, open and unconcerned.
(*Spectator*, I, 137)

Yet into this mock-real world Steele incorporates the conflict,
which spurs the reader's interest, and a measure of character interaction that is credible. A young man sees Laetitia one day and
falls desperately in love, to no avail. She remains cool. This conflict is resolved quickly: "He still Sighed in vain for *Laetitia*, but
found certain Relief in the agreeable Conversation of *Daphne*"
(*Spectator*, I, 138). Steele's technique of relating some—and having Mr. Spectator report some—of the conversation provides additional realism and credibility during the essential confrontation
in the story:

> . . . he one Day told [Daphne], that he had something to say
> to her he hoped she would be pleased with.—*Faith* Daphne, con-
> tinued he, *I am in Love with thee, and despise thy Sister sin-*
> *cerely.* The manner of his declaring himself gave his Mistress
> occasion for a very hearty Laughter. —*Nay*, says he, *I knew you*
> *would Laugh at me, but I'll ask your Father.* He did so; the
> Father received his Intelligence with no less Joy than Surprize,
> and was very glad he had now no Care left but for his *Beauty,*
> which he thought he could carry to Market at his Leisure.
> (*Spectator*, I, 138)

Thus, while the sudden shift in the man's affections is rather humorous and Laetitia's actions are satirically exaggerated, the concluding remarks of the father about Laetitia's future and his joy
are quite ironic. One can imagine the head of the household sitting around the morning tea table, *Spectator* in hand, nodding his
approval as he reads Mr. Spectator's moral conclusion to his family: "As it is an Argument of a light Mind, to think the worse of
our selves for the Imperfections of our Persons, it is equally below us to value our selves upon the Advantages of them" (*Spec-*
tator, I, 138).

The technique of insisting on the truth of the domestic story to
be told in order to heighten its appeal as an example in a family

is found also in Steele's "Honoria and Flavia" (No. 91). Mr. Spectator at the beginning says,

> I cannot forbear inserting the Circumstances which pleased me in the Account a young Lady gave me of the Loves of a Family in Town, which shall be nameless, or rather for the better Sound, and Elevation of the History, instead of Mr. and Mrs. such a one, I shall call them by feigned Names. (*Spectator*, I, 384)

But this insistence on the truth of the episode does not make the characters succeed as individuals; they exist wholly to feed the satire and the theme as recognized through action. The description of the two by Mr. Spectator reveals them to be typical mother-daughter rivals:

> The agreeable *Flavia* would be what she is not, as well as her Mother *Honoria,* but all their Beholders are more partial to an Affectation of what a Person is growing up to, than of what has been already enjoyed, and is gone for ever. It is therefore allowed to *Flavia* to look forward, but not to *Honoria* to look back. . . . and as *Honoria* has given *Flavia* to understand, that it is ill bred to be always calling Mother, *Flavia* is as well pleased never to be called Child. (*Spectator*, I, 385)

These two papier-mâché characters function in an episodic plot designed to show them—and their kind—at their worst. We see them at each other's throats at the play, but most humorous are their derring-does with the perennial beaux Tom Tulip and Dick Crastin. The humor of their behavior is equalled by the irony of their opinions about their importance and by the satirical tone Mr. Spectator uses in portraying the scene.

The same technique that Steele used to introduce "Honoria and Flavia," and his effort to establish the credibility of his didactic apologue, are readily apparent in Addison's "Eudoxus and Leontine" (No. 123). "This makes me often think on a Story I have heard of two friends," Mr. Spectator says, "which I shall give my Reader at large, under feigned Names." And he continues, "The

Moral of it may, I hope, be useful, though there are some Circumstances which make it rather appear like a Novel, than a true Story" (*Spectator,* I, 502). What makes it "appear like a Novel" is the story's excellently complex plot, which is a sentimental, positive example of how to rear children. Two old friends, Eudoxus (rich in material things) and Leontine (rich in intellectual powers) marry late in life and have a son and daughter respectively.

> As they were one Day talking together with their usual Intimacy, *Leontine,* considering how incapable he was of giving his Daughter a proper Education in his own House [his wife had died], and *Eudoxus* reflecting on the ordinary Behaviour of a Son who knows himself to be the Heir of a great Estate, they both agreed upon an Exchange of Children, namely that the Boy should be bred up with *Leontine* as his Son, and that the Girl should live with *Eudoxus* as his Daughter, till they were each of them arrived at Years of Discretion. (*Spectator,* I, 503)

The plan works beautifully, for Florio (the boy) and Leonilla (the girl) both grow up unspoiled and educated in the proper spheres. The conclusion brings the resolution of the "secret" and a happy ending, amidst a flood of tears:

> *Florio* was so overwhelmed with this Profusion of Happiness, that he was not able to make a Reply, but threw himself down at his Father's Feet, and amidst a flood of Tears, kissed and embraced his Knees, asking his Blessing, and expressing in dumb show those Sentiments of Love, Duty and Gratitude that were too big for Utterance. (*Spectator,* I, 505)

"To conclude," interposes Mr. Spectator, "the happy Pair were married, and half *Eudoxus*'s Estate settled upon them. *Leontine* and *Eudoxus* passed the Remainder of their Lives together, and received in the dutiful and affectionate Behaviour of *Florio* and *Leonilla* the just Recompence, as well as the natural Effects, of that Care which they had bestowed upon them in their Educa-

tion" (*Spectator*, I, 505). Perhaps none of Addison's Saturday
sermons did so much as this purely sentimental domestic apologue. As an example of its kind, the story of "Eudoxus and Leontine" is well developed.

In No. 128 Mr. Spectator relates a domestic apologue, which is
hardly more than an anecdote, to illustrate the complementary na-
tures of men and women. Specifically, his point is that women
"find that they choose rather to associate themselves with a Person
who resembles them in that light and volatile Humour which is
natural to them, than to such as are qualified to moderate and
counter-ballance it" (*Spectator*, II, 9). At first he is content to
exemplify his idea by alluding to the anecdote about Faustina,
Marcus Aurelius' wife, who loved gladiators so much that her son,
Commodus, was interested only in contests and fighting for prizes
when he became emperor. But since he is in the country at this
time, Mr. Spectator then turns to the contemporary scene to supply the material for further illustration. "A Country Couple" is
neither developed in plot nor characterization, but the theme is
appropriate, and he does achieve some credibility of description,
mainly through the use of a precise vocabulary of country terms.

Briefly, the narrative concerns a woman who likes the town,
a man who likes the country, and children who are therefore dis-
concerted: the boys look down on the mother, the girls think the
father is a clown. The balanced style artificially enhances the balanced situation. And the subject matter is superbly integrated into
the situation Mr. Spectator finds himself in—a man of the town
observing the hopes and ambitions of country folk.

While in the country, Sir Roger and Mr. Spectator stopped one
day to have their fortunes told by gypsies. Sir Roger had said
some rather testy things about gypsies and their communal exis-
tence, and this gives Mr. Spectator an opportunity to present them
in a more favorable light, and he seizes the chance:

> I might here entertain my Reader with historical Remarks on
> this idle profligate People. . . . But instead of entering into

Observations of this Nature, I shall fill the remaining Part of my Paper with a Story which is still fresh in *Holland,* and was printed in one of our Monthly Accounts about twenty Years ago. (*Spectator,* II, 17)[18]

The story itself fits in well with the previous discussions of gypsies with Sir Roger; it is about a poor but intelligent "gypsy" boy who is compassionately taken on a steamer by a benevolent merchant, who turns out to be the boy's lost father. The discovery of kinship here is handled much less sentimentally than in "Eudoxus and Leontine" (No. 123) and the reactions of joy are generally restrained, straightforward, and natural:

> The Lad was very well pleased to find a Father, who was so rich, and likely to leave him a good Estate; the Father, on the other Hand, was not a little delighted to see a Son return to him, whom he had given for lost, with such a Strength of Constitution, Sharpness of Understanding, and Skill in Languages. (*Spectator,* II, 18)

The gypsy, implies Addison, can do things as well as anyone if he is not chained to his environment. The fact that Mr. Spectator leads the reader to think he is being merely entertained helps him arrive at the point with greater subtlety. Actually, of course, it is an old trick that adds variety to Addison's and Steele's method of handling the material in the domestic apologue. No. 130 is part of a number of issues concerning Mr. Spectator and Sir Roger, serials (of which this story was one result) that make up a running narrative that can be considered a cumulative episode.

One of the most sentimental of Addison's domestic apologues is his "Constantia and Theodosius" (No. 164), a story that satirizes the cruel practice of fathers' arranging marriages for their daughters with financial gain rather than love as the foundation. Much attention is given to plot development and character motivation. Addison uses a letter from Theodosius to show his feelings first hand. Constantia's anguish when she discovers that Theodosius has entered a monastery, thinking she is to be married to another, is poignantly drawn. Constantia enters a nunnery, and the most dramatic moment in the apologue occurs when she confesses to Father Francis, who actually is Theodosius. The dramatic irony is quite effective, though the situation is perhaps too sentimental for modern taste. Mr. Spectator says that when she died her request to be buried beside Theodosius was granted. "Their Tombs are still to be seen," claims Mr. Spectator, "with a short Latin Inscription over them to the following Purpose. Here lie the Bodies of Father *Francis* and Sister *Constance. They were lovely in their Lives, and in their Deaths they were not divided*" (*Spectator,* II, 148).[19] The apologue is unified in theme, limited in characterization, substantial in plot, constructed with limited action, and well written, entertaining, and instructive.

Addison turns to *The Works of Josephus* for his next domestic apologue, which occurs in No. 171 and is entitled "Mariamne and Herod" (See *Spectator,* II, 176*n*). The narrative gives useful advice on how to live with a jealous husband. Noteworthy is how the story (jealous Herod's orders, when he leaves, to kill Mariamne if she is unfaithful, etc.) develops several sides or effects of the struggle with jealousy. Furthermore, it is interesting to observe that this story comes at the end of an extended discussion of jealousy over several issues (Nos. 169-71). Mr. Spectator closes a related unit, as is frequently the case, with a piece of prose fiction. Never does he go long without telling a story, and his short stories are an integral part of the structure of his essays. In this instance, "Mariamne and Herod" is the means to imagize the idea (Jealousy).

Such is also the case with Mr. Spectator's analysis of education, which "when it works upon a noble Mind, draws out to View every latent Vertue and Perfection, which without such Helps are never able to make their Appearance" (*Spectator,* II, 338). He concludes with the sentimental love story of "The Barbados Negroes" (No. 215). Again, there is the avowal that the story is true, although no source has been found:

Since I am engaged on this Subject, I cannot forbear mentioning a Story which I have lately heard, and which is so well attested, that I have no manner of reason to suspect the Truth of it. I may call it a kind of wild Tragedy that passed about twelve Years ago at St. *Christophers,* one of our *British* Leeward Islands. (*Spectator,* II, 339)

Then economically the story of two Negroes in love with the same beauty is related. The conflict is resolved by the killing of the girl, and a witness's observations are recorded:

A Slave who was at his Work not far from the Place where this astonishing piece of Cruelty was committed, hearing the Shrieks of the dying Person, ran to see what was the Occasion of them. He there discovered the Woman lying dead upon the Ground, with the two Negroes on each side of her, kissing the dead Corps, weeping over it, and beating their Breasts in the utmost Agonies of Grief and Despair. He immediately ran to the *English* Family with the News of what he had seen; who upon coming to the Place saw the Woman dead, and the two Negroes expiring by her with Wounds they had given themselves. (*Spectator,* II, 340)

Sentimental and tragic, as a dramatic concentration of his ideas on education "The Barbados Negroes" surely was welcomed as a valuable part of the tea equipage. Readers of every age and station could easily appreciate more fully the "unspeakable Blessing to be born in those Parts of the World where Wisdom and Knowledge flourish . . ." (*Spectator,* II, 340).

Steele's "Father and Son" (No. 426) has as its theme "the Care of Parents due to their Children, and the Piety of Children towards their Parents" (*Spectator,* III, 597). It is one of Steele's most highly developed narratives and incorporates the eastern elixir of life motif with the conflict among three generations of fathers and sons. Basilius possessed a small "Phial" that "collected such Powers, as shall revive the Springs of Life when they are yet but just ceased" (*Spectator,* III, 598), but upon his death his fun-loving son Alexandrinus fails to administer the elixir. Alexandrinus in due time, learning a lesson from his own ways, tells his son Renatus that his body will turn to gold if the magic potion is applied soon after his demise. The force of the narrative comes in the irony of the conclusion; the biter is bit when Renatus follows his instructions as a good son ought:

> Well, *Alexandrinus* died, and the Heir of his body (as our Term is) could not forbear, in the Wantonnesses of his Heart, to measure the Length and Breadth of his beloved Father, and cast up the ensuing Value of him before he proceeded to Operation. When he knew the immense Reward of his Pains, he began the Work: But lo! when he had anointed the Corps all over, and began to apply the Liquor, the Body stirr'd, and *Renatus,* in a Fright, broke the Phial. (*Spectator,* III, 600)[20]

The surprise ending marks humorously the inevitability of poetic justice. After his story, Mr. Spectator rightly sees no need to draw the moral.

As indicated by the preceding examination of the domestic apologue in the *Spectator,* the form usually has a sentimental nature that provides an excellent medium for instruction. Yet as employed by Addison and Steele the form is often characterized by an equal mixture of humor, satire, and irony. Approaches to the narratives are as varied as the subject matter and the methods of narration; sometimes they occur almost alone as the whole of an issue, and on other occasions the apologues either introduce a subject or conclude a topic discussed over several days. The narratives are quite strong in plot structure and in their adherence to a tightly controlled theme, and, while the characters are usually not individualized to any great extent, they are nevertheless vividly drawn forces who demand the reader's interest and attention. The authors as a rule insist on the truth of their account, for they never lose sight of the fact that the domestic apologue would be of particular value "to all well regulated Families."

OTHERS

It is possible in a sense to place the remaining significant short narratives into one category and call it the exemplum, for they are short anecdotes or stories used to point a moral or sustain an argument. But doing this, in another sense, presupposes that the other narratives as a whole do not belong under the broad heading of exemplum, and we have seen that many of the stories of Mr. Spectator "point a moral or sustain an argument." Furthermore, placing a number of narratives under one heading presupposes a similarity in technique, method of handling, and structure that the remaining stories do not have. If it is understood, however, that the stories—which do not have characteristics calling for them to be listed and discussed under previous categories—have as a common purpose to illustrate and to instruct, then the exemplum is the generic form into which they most nearly fit. The narratives in this category invariably are preceded by a stated moral, which they illustrate. As a form the exemplum has, of course, an ancient heritage, being particularly popular in medieval sermons, and its appearance in the *Spectator* indicates still further the varied scope of the short story in the work. The more important examples of this kind of story in the *Spectator* are Steele's "Old Man in Athens" (No. 6), Addison's "Glaphyra" from Josephus (No. 110), Budgell's "Old Man in Coffee-House" (No. 150), Addison's "Eugenius" (No. 177), Martyn's [?] two anecdotes from Plutarch's *Life of Pyrrhus* (No. 180), Addison's "Boccalini's Traveller" (No. 355), Steele's "A Dauphin of France" (No. 382), and "Bussy d'Amboise" (No. 467).[21]

Spectator No. 6 opens with the statement, "I know no Evil under the Sun so great as the Abuse of the Understanding, and yet there is no one Vice more common" (*Spectator*, I, 28). This is the main topic of the day, and Mr. Spectator elaborates upon it at length, framing it around a conversation he had one night with Sir Roger. Mr. Spectator finally remarks that this abuse of the understanding is most readily noticeable in people's views of older

persons. It is at this point that he introduces the brief exemplum
as a capstone to the entire essay:

> Respect to all kind of Superiours is founded methinks upon
> Instinct; and yet what is so ridiculous as Age? I make this abrupt
> Transition to the Mention of this Vice more than any other, in
> order to introduce a little Story, which I think a pretty Instance
> that the most polite Age is in danger of being the most vicious.
> (*Spectator*, I, 30) [22]

The anecdote is related economically in one tightly knit paragraph. An old man goes to the theatre in Athens where the Athenians play a joke on him and refuse to give him a seat. The Lace-
demonians rise and give him a place to sit, whereupon the Athenians, probably with a sense of guilt, applaud. The epigrammatic
finish goes straight to the heart of the matter that had been introduced at the beginning of the essay: " '. . . and the old Man
cry'd out, *The* Athenians *understand what is good, but the* Lace-
demonians *practice it* '" (*Spectator*, 1, 31). [23] The story is a sterling
illustration of the exposition. We get only a brief glimpse of the
old man, but it is an unforgettable one.

The exact structure as noticed above is followed by Addison in
No. 110, where again Mr. Spectator reports a discussion with Sir
Roger (concerning the philosophy of John Locke). The immor-
tality of the soul is indeed a learned subject, so Mr. Spectator
turns to the exemplum for help:

> I shall dismiss this Paper with a Story out of *Josephus*, not so
> much for the Sake of the Story it self, as for the moral Reflections
> with which the Author concludes it, and which I shall here set
> down in his own Words. (*Spectator*, I, 455)

The story itself is a mere incident, and it might have been included in the category of dream vision if it had been more fully
developed:

> "*Glaphyra* the Daughter of King *Archilaus*, after the Death of

her two first Husbands (being married to a third, who was Brother to her first Husband, and so passionately in Love with her that he turn'd off his former Wife to make Room for this Marriage) had a very odd kind of Dream. She fancied that she saw her first Husband coming towards her, and that she embraced him with great Tenderness; when in the Midst of the Pleasure which she expressed at the Sight of him, he reproached her after the following Manner: *Glaphyra,* says he, thou hast made good the old Saying, That Women are not to be trusted. Was not I the Husband of thy Virginity? have I not Children by thee? How couldst thou forget our Loves so far as to enter into a second Marriage, and after that into a third, nay to take for thy Husband a Man who has so shamelessly crept into the Bed of his Brother? However, for the Sake of our passed Loves, I shall free thee from thy present Reproach, and make thee mine for ever. *Glaphyra* told this Dream to several Women of her Acquaintance, and died soon after." (*Spectator,* I, 455–56)

Only the words spoken by the husband to Glaphyra save the anecdote from being a rather clumsy concentration of facts. Nevertheless, the quotation of the whole story serves to illustrate the average length of these exempla and to indicate how they provide an imaginative summation of the preceding thoughts.

In *Spectator* No. 152 Steele's exemplum entitled "Military Men" illustrates not an abstract idea but exemplifies, with superb irony, the contention that "There is no sort of People whose Conversation is so pleasant as that of military Men . . ." (*Spectator,* II, 96). Upon being informed that his bosom military friend had drowned crossing a river on a ferryboat with his horse, a soldier "very gravely replyed, *Ay he had a mad Horse*" (*Spectator,* II, 98). Such an extreme, and humorously ironical, illustration is also used by Addison in No. 177, an essay that advances the theory that charity should be exercised with prudence and caution. Announcing gravely that "This may possibly be explained better by an Example than by a Rule," Mr. Spectator tells about Eugenius' habit of walking instead of riding and giving his fare to a beggar (*Spectator,* II, 198–99). "Boccalini's Traveller" (No. 355) in like man-

ner comically extends Mr. Spectator's resolute ideas about ignor-
ing critics. The traveller was so pestered with the noise of grasshoppers that he alighted from his horse in great wrath to kill them
all; he was troubling himself to no avail, for they would have died
themselves in a few weeks and he would have suffered nothing
from them (*Spectator*, III, 325).[24] Thus, the exemplum is sometimes used to extend an argument and point a moral in a lively
ironical and humorous way.

Sentimentality, on the other hand, is the chief characteristic of
Steele's "A Dauphin of France" (No. 382) and "Bussy d'Amboise"
(No. 467). In method and technique they are not unusual. Both
are quite brief. The subject of the former number is the atone-
ment of a man in acknowledgment of a fault. The story of a Dauphin of France who gave a wrong order, insisted on its execution,
and was sent to make amends to the proper officer is calculated
to cause all those readers with faults to make a clean breast of
things. Likewise, the account of Bussy d'Amboise, who appeared
at a magnificent affair in plain clothes and received all the attention, quite effectively draws the point of the essay on the love of
praise.[25]

It is not so much the refinement of the narrative or the original-
ity of the plot or the portrayal of characters that often concerns
Mr. Spectator; rather, as a means to convert an idea into a sense
perception, illustrative short narratives achieve a prominent place.
By scattering innumerable illustrative anecdotes throughout the
Spectator, many so brief that they defy listing or naming as individual narratives, the authors continually emphasize the fact that
Mr. Spectator—preacher, critic, philosopher, observer, and pedant
—is first and last a storyteller.

7

Conclusions

> It is common with me to run from Book to Book to exercise my
> Mind with many Objects, and qualify my self for my daily La-
> bours. After an Hour . . . something will remain to be Food to
> the Imagination. The Writings that please me most on such Oc-
> casions are Stories. . . .
>
> —Mr. Spectator, *Spectator* No. 491

Mr. Spectator was admittedly fond of stories, and what attracted
him he apparently suspected was universal enough to appeal to
his readers as well. The success of the *Spectator* suggests that he
was right; for in this periodical the authors never go long without
relating a short narrative "to exercise [the] Mind" and to "please"
the soul. Indeed, such "Food to the Imagination" is almost daily
fare (*Spectator*, IV, 240). The short story occupies a central position in the master plan "to enliven Morality with Wit, and to
temper Wit with Morality, that [the] Readers may, if possible,
both Ways find their Account in the Speculation of the Day"
(*Spectator*, I, 44).

As the foregoing chapters disclose, the *Spectator*, far more than
is generally thought, is a virtual storehouse of short fiction, con-
taining approximately one hundred distinct stories and anecdotes
with definite narrative qualities. Scattered throughout the 555
original issues, they not only constantly reinforce the fictional
point of view of the putative author but also expand the point of
view by introducing other narrators either by direct contact with
Mr. Spectator or via letter. The overriding characteristic of the

short story in the *Spectator* is the variety of types that are represented; readers seeking something new and uncommon could always find it. A classification of the story types establishes the fact beyond question, for the narratives make up nine categories of short fiction (and the authors reveal their artistic sophistication by sometimes combining several forms, as in "The Vision of Mirzah"). Perhaps the following expression of fictional theory by Mr. Spectator in No. 538 explains why he valued variety so highly:

> Surprize is so much the Life of Stories, that every one aims at it who endeavours to please by telling them. Smooth Delivery, an elegant Choice of Words, and a sweet Arrangement, are all beautifying *Graces,* but not the Particulars in this Point of Conversation which either long command the Attention, or strike with the Violence of a sudden Passion, or occasion the Burst of Laughter which accompanies Humour.

"I have sometimes fancy'd," he continues,

> that the Mind is in this Case like a Traveller who sees a fine Seat in Haste; he acknowledges the Delightfulness of a Walk set with Regularity, but wou'd be uneasy if he were oblig'd to pace it over, when the first View had let him into all its Beauties from one End to the other. (*Spectator,* IV, 420–21)

In addition, of course, the editors were shrewd enough to recognize the practicality of variety if they were to attract and hold an audience with a multiplicity of interests and backgrounds.[1] As Mr. Spectator himself notes in No. 179, "Were I always Grave one half of my Readers would fall off from me: Were I always Merry I should lose the other" (*Spectator,* II, 204).

The emphasis on variety does not mean, however, that the short narratives in the *Spectator* lack, on the whole, those beautifying graces "Smooth Delivery, an elegant Choice of Words, and a sweet Arrangement." One especially recalls the dream vision "The Vision of Mirzah" (No. 159) with its adroit exposition and dialogue, its point of view that superbly conveys the difference be-

tween the real and ideal worlds, and its use of vocabulary to enhance the oriental atmosphere. And a sweet arrangement and a
tight unity of ideas are exemplified best in the Character "The
Envious Man" (No. 19) and in the fables, although it is everywhere evident that close organization and attention to one dominant, controlling theme are always remarkable traits of Mr. Spectator's stories and his correspondents' accounts.

Seldom, if ever, does a short narrative occur that exists for its
own sake, for the announced dual purpose of the *Spectator* is
never abandoned. The short fiction invariably has a didactic function, either implicit or explicit, and the narratives—particularly
the fable, domestic apologue, and exemplum—usually illustrate
an idea or proposition. "There is nothing in Nature more irksom
than general Discourses, especially when they turn chiefly upon
Words," Mr. Spectator writes in No. 267 (*Spectator*, II, 537).
Therefore the narrators present short stories, which occasionally
masquerade as "true accounts," to image the abstract. An added
dividend naturally accrues when such a "pretty Instance" also
"alleviate[s] the Severity" (*Spectator*, I, 382) of a number and en-
tertains the reader by taking "off from that Satiety we are apt
to complain of in our usual and ordinary Entertainments" (*Spectator*, III, 541).

Furthermore, by writing narratives representing so many different story types Mr. Spectator clearly hoped to develop the taste
of his readers for "widely different dishes" (*Spectator*, I, 389) and
to whet their curiosity when they sat down to read the daily paper. Thus, in the course of the *Spectator* the authors attempt not
only to improve the taste of the reader but also to cater to it.
Constant is the effort to keep the didacticism from becoming op-
pressive, but insofar as the *Spectator* is concerned Joseph Bunn
Heidler's statement that the "ostensible aim of prose fiction in the
period from 1700 to 1719 continued to be realistic portrayal for
ethical ends" is indisputable.[2] Mr. Spectator's intentions—which
his practice fails to belie—are a matter of record: ". . . and if there
be any use in these my Papers, it is this, that without represent-

ing Vice under any false alluring Notions, they give my Reader
an Insight into the Ways of Men, and represent Human Nature in
all its changeable Colours" (*Spectator*, II, 450).

Most impressive indeed is the evidence in the *Spectator* of its
authors' abilities to garner a wide range of types into a cohesive
whole. But perhaps more important still is the evidence in the
stories themselves that indicates to what extent the authors varied
and shaped old forms (Character, fable, fabliau, exemplum, for
example) and newer types (oriental tale, rogue literature, mock-
sentimental tale, for example) to their own needs. The Character, of which forty-odd examples occur, is not merely treated in
the traditional manner; Mr. Spectator and his cohorts elasticize
and individualize the types through character interaction, names,
dialogue, detailed description, specific settings, and the technique
of concentrating less on numerous aspects of a type and more on
the primary traits of a named person. The twenty-three fables
attest to the narrator's gift of employing a form both in narrative
episodes and in his expository essays in order to promote the
didactic purpose in an entertaining manner. As with the Character, the fables are of several varieties—eastern, allegorical, and
traditional animal—and the approach and methods of handling
are seldom predictable. The seventeen dream visions-cum-allegory
are outstanding cases of the translation of ideas into images, and
whether presented for literary, moral, or political reasons they
show conscious craftsmanship and artistic skill. Satirical as well as
sentimental, narrated by correspondents as well as by Mr. Spectator, episodic as well as continuous accounts of a single
action, extensively developed as well as economically brief, the
dream vision-cum-allegory represents a successful endeavor "to
revive that way of Writing" (*Spectator*, IV, 275). The fifteen examples of oriental and eastern material, discussed in Chapter 5,
are particularly enlightening and interesting for their emphasis
on plot, the creation of an atmosphere of exotic fantasy, and
brilliant setting. The miscellaneous forms are used often as
satirical vehicles, especially the mock-sentimental and satirical ad-

venture stories, the fabliau and rogue literature, and the domestic apologue. The authors breathe new life into the exemplum; by using various narrators to shift the point of view and by choosing appropriately vivid and realistic incidents, the form constantly exposes its changing colors.

The narratives that Sir Richard Steele contributed to the *Spectator* are by and large more sentimental than Addison's (though, interestingly enough, Steele wrote the single mock-sentimental tale), and Steele wrote most of the stories of a domestic nature. Steele also was the instigating force behind a majority of the numbers that employ the letter device, and it may be assumed that Addison felt more comfortable behind the mask of Mr. Spectator than did his colleague. Although a number of Steele's early narratives show the results of haste in their weak development, later he incorporated the letter device more smoothly into his fictional work and paid more attention to plot motivation and character interaction and dialogue (see Nos. 426, 436, and 491). Steele was prone to look to contemporary events for subject matter, whereas Addison drew largely on his classical background.

Addison could be sentimental, too, but he tried to restrain the impulse with the fiction that he was presenting facts and "truth" without prejudice. Addison is especially successful in imaging a scene, and his developing techniques in this area can be detected by comparing "Publick Credit" (No. 3) with "The Vision of Mirzah" (No. 159). By making no attempt as a rule to keep the various types separate, many of Addison's stories contain a pleasing mixture of elements, as the oriental material, allegory, and dream vision in "The Vision of Mirzah" indicate. Addison's narratives may be criticized for oftentimes being too artificially introduced; but the narratives, even the ones with very summary treatment, are invariably well organized around a "single action, with unity of mood and strict limitation of characters."[3] Much of the atmosphere and tone of his narratives, the oriental material in particular, is due to names and objects mentioned in a basically English situation rather than to eastern philosophy, landscape, or characters. Yet Addison popularized such fantasies with a public still skeptical about fiction, and Watson maintains that Addison's influence on the oriental tale "was achieved by his casual use of oriental material as illustrations for some half-dozen of his moral discussions."[4] Addison brought forth new forms, therefore, as well as old ones. As an anonymous letterwriter told Mr. Spectator in No. 158:

> "I have observed through the whole Course of your Rhapsodies, (as you once very well called them) you are very industrious to overthrow all that many [of] your Superiours who have gone before you have made their Rule of writing." (*Spectator*, II, 118)

His narratives in the *Spectator* serve as a kind of Aristotelian catharsis, which he suggested (in his "On Histories," 1710) was necessary in fiction:

> inventions of this kind are like food and exercise to a good natured disposition, which they please and gratify at the same time that they nourish and strenghten. The greater the affliction is in which we see our favourites in these relations engaged, the greater is the pleasure we take in seeing them relieved.[5]

This study of the short fiction in the *Spectator* demonstrates anew the artistry of its contents and the amazing flexibility of its plan. However familiar the story types, the narratives and anecdotes emerge generally as new and uncommon refreshment and instruction. The motto for *Spectator* No. 1 promised:

> Not smoke after flame does he plan to give, but after smoke the light, that then he may set forth striking and wondrous tales. (*Spectator*, I, 1)

The hope was made reality, the light of imagination was diffused throughout by striking and wondrous narratives, and possibly for this reason the *Spectator* became the most widely read and best periodical of the early eighteenth century.[6]

Notes

INTRODUCTION

[1] Joseph Addison, Richard Steele, and others, *The Spectator*, ed. Donald F. Bond (Oxford: The Clarendon Press, 1965), I, 244–45. Bond's five-volume edition is the edition used throughout and is hereafter cited in the text as "*Spectator*" and appropriate volume number.

[2] For a list of the various editions and their merits and demerits, see Bond's *Spectator*, I, v–ix. John Hampden in 1966 edited an edition for the Folio Society.

[3] Benjamin Boyce, "English Short Fiction in the Eighteenth Century: A Preliminary View," *Studies in Short Fiction*, 5 (Winter 1968), 95.

[4] John Gay, *The Present State of Wit (1711)*, Augustan Reprint Society, 1st series, No. 3 (Ann Arbor: Edwards Brothers, 1947), pp. 4, 6.

[5] Samuel Johnson, *Life of Addison* in his *Lives of the English Poets*, ed. George Birkbeck Hill (Oxford: The Clarendon Press, 1905), II, 92–93, 96.

[6] Thomas Babington Macaulay, *The Works of Lord Macaulay* (New York: Longmans, Green and Co., 1900), VII, 97–98. Macaulay lauds the naturalness of the episodes, and he says that the narrative connecting the essays, which "was indeed constructed with no art or labour," gave the readers their first taste of "untried pleasure." He adds, hastily, that such "events can hardly be said to form a plot" (VII, 97).

[7] A comprehensive survey of twentieth-century critical remarks on the *Spectator* is not, of course, attempted here, but the student or reader should note that critical appraisal relating to the short fiction may be found in a number of places: in studies of the essay, especially as it is represented in the periodicals of the eighteenth century; in studies of the essay as a literary form; in Benjamin Boyce's "English Short Fiction in the Eighteenth Century: A Preliminary View," pp. 95–112; and in Donald F. Bond's Introduction to the 1965 Oxford Edition of the *Spectator*. In articles on specialized aspects of the *Spectator* limited attention is sometimes given to fictional features that do not conveniently fall into several of the schemes indicated above. See Rae Blanchard, "Richard Steele's Maryland Story," *American Quarterly*, 10 (1958), 78–82; Robert D. Chambers, "Addison at Work on the *Spec-*

tator," *Modern Philology*, 56 (1959), 145–53; Margaret Turner, "The Influence of La Bruyère on the 'Tatler' and the 'Spectator,'" *Modern Language Review*, 48 (1953), 10–16; and especially Melvin R. Watson's excellent study entitled "The 'Spectator' Tradition and the Development of the Familiar Essay," *ELH*, 13 (1946), 189–215. Professor Donald Roberts Simpson has also made a useful and significant contribution to *Spectator* scholarship, and I strongly recommend that his work be consulted; his work, *The Spectator Reconsidered* (Ann Arbor: University Microfilms, 1962), was a doctoral dissertation at the University of Colorado.

⁸ Henry Seidel Canby, *The Short Story in English* (New York: Henry Holt and Co., 1909), p. 180.

⁹ Cf. J. H. Millar's *The Mid-Eighteenth Century* (New York: Charles Scribner's Sons, 1902), p. 126.

¹⁰ Canby, pp. 177–78.

¹¹ Canby, p. 178.

¹² Canby, p. 180–81.

¹³ Canby, p. 182.

¹⁴ Canby, p. 182.

¹⁵ Robert D. Mayo, *The English Novel in the Magazines, 1740–1815* (Evanston, Ill.: Northwestern Univ. Press, 1962), p. 431.

¹⁶ Ray B. West, Jr. *The Short Story in America* (Freeport, N.Y.: Books for Libraries Press, 1952), p. 2.

¹⁷ Frank O'Connor, *The Lonely Voice: A Study of the Short Story* (Cleveland and New York: The World Publishing Co, 1963), p. 27.

¹⁸ Lionel Stevenson, *The English Novel: A Panorama* (Boston: Houghton Mifflin Co., 1960), p. 6.

¹⁹ Boyce, "English Short Fiction in the Eighteenth Century," p. 97.

²⁰ Simpson, p. 57.

²¹ Stevenson, p. 13.

²² Stevenson, pp. 15–16.

²³ Mayo, p. 34.

CHAPTER 1

¹ See John Colin Dunlop, *History of Prose Fiction*, rev. Henry Wilson, 2 vols. (London: George Bell & Sons, 1896.)

² The tales attributed to Bidpai, supposed to be upwards of two thousand years old, exemplify this phenomenon remarkably: his book, called *Hitopadesa* (wholesome instruction), was first written in an Indian language and was translated into Persian at the end of the sixth

century and later into Syriac, then into Arabic, and still later there were Greek, Latin, Hebrew, German, Spanish, and Italian versions, generally called *Kalilah ve Dimnah*. The Italian version was translated into English by Sir Thomas North in 1570 and the Syriac version into more literal English by Keith Falconer in 1885. Such a transition from country to country makes it less surprising that the *Spectator* contains numerous stories of ancient origin. See Dunlop, II, 4–6.

3 See *Short Fiction of the Seventeenth Century,* ed. Charles C. Mish (New York: New York Univ. Press, 1963).

4 This was probably written in England in Latin around 1300.

5 See *Elizabethan Tales,* ed. Edward J. O'Brien (London: George Allen & Unwin, 1937), p. 20.

6 Mish, p. [vii].

7 Mish, p. [vii].

8 Mish, p. xiii-xiv.

9 Mish, p. xvi.

10 Quoted by George Sherburn, "The Restoration and the Eighteenth Century, 1660–1789," in *A Literary History of England,* ed. Albert C. Baugh (New York: Appleton-Century-Crofts, 1948), 802–03.

11 (New York: Oxford Univ. Press, 1926), p. 61.

12 A number of periodicals from 1690 to 1710—such as the *British Apollo, Memoirs for the Ingenious,* and the *Compleat Library*—that contain little or no fiction have either not been mentioned or not discussed in this survey. I have examined all of the significant periodicals of the period, and the selection, it is believed, reflects those that have contributed the most to the history of the short story and the novel, too.

13 See Graham, *The Beginnings of English Literary Periodicals,* pp. 15–16.

14 Chapter I of Mayo's *The English Novel in the Magazines, 1740–1815,* pp. 11–69, relates the magazine tradition in prose fiction up to 1740 and has some worthwhile general comments on the priod 1690-1710. I am indebted to Professor Mayo for his stimulating ideas and organized groupings of the periodicals.

15 The first number was entitled *The Athenian Gazette;* or, *Casuistical Mercury.* Separate numbers afterwards were called the *Athenian Mercury.*

16 "Advertisement," *The Supplement* to the first volume of the *Athenian Gazette* (London, 1691), p. [iv]. Quoted by Mayo, p. 16.

17 *Athenian Mercury,* I, No. 23, Quest. 2.

18 *Athenian Mercury,* II, No. 11, Quest. 1.

19 *Athenian Mercury,* III, No. 3, Quest. 2.

[20] For more information on the influence on the novel proper, see Mayo, pp. 17–18.

[21] *Athenian Oracle,* I (London, 1703–10), 110.

[22] Mayo, p. 19. Defoe's *Review* (19 Feb. 1704–11 June 1713) and its department called "*Mercure Scandale:* or, Advice from the Scandalous Club" (lasting from Feb. 1704 to April 1705) answered questions from readers in a much more serious way than Dunton, but Defoe probably got the idea for the feature from Dunton. Inquiries from readers in the *Review,* and the *Little Review,* often reveal narrative elements contained in the *Athenian Mercury* inquiries and later carried on in letters to Mr. Spectator. See Majorie Nicolson's Introduction to William L. Payne's *The Best of Defoe's Review* (New York: Columbia Univ. Press, 1951), pp. xiii–xiv.

[23] See the *Gentleman's Journal,* No. 1 (Jan. 1692), p. 1.

[24] *Gentleman's Journal,* No. 1 (Jan. 1692), Sig. A2v.

[25] *Gentleman's Journal,* No. 1 (Jan. 1692), pp. 23–27.

[26] *Gentleman's Journal,* No. 2 (Feb. 1692), pp. 4–5.

[27] *Gentleman's Journal,* No. 6 (June 1692), p. 8. Also note the application at the end of "The Jealous Husbands" in No. 7 (July 1692), p. 6; and the illustrative story of manners in "The Reward of Indifference," No. 8 (Aug. 1692), p. 3.

[28] *Gentleman's Journal,* No. 4 (April 1692), pp. 4–6.

[29] *Gentleman's Journal,* No. 10 (Oct. 1692), pp. 2–5. The summary is mine.

[30] *Gentleman's Journal,* No. 14 (Feb. 1693), pp. 46–47.

[31] *Gentleman's Journal,* No. 15 (March 1693), pp. 76–78.

[32] *Gentleman's Journal,* No. 16 (April 1693), pp. 115–18.

[33] Robert Wieder, *Pierre Motteux et les Debuts du Journalisme en Angleterre au XVII siècle: Le Gentleman's Journal (1692–1694)* (Paris: n.d.), p. 105 (translation mine): Vingt années environ avant le *Spectateur,* le *Gentleman's Journal,* séduisant microcosme, révèle à travers ses chroniques souvent badines, un esprit d'ardente recherche que se construit et qui mûrit; le journalisme naissant s'affinera certes encore; mais avec Motteux on voit déjà la part active qu'il prenda désormais à la vie intellectuelle de la nation. Car il prétend, à juste titre, se faire le miroir de la "melior pars" du pays, de cette classe qui, sans qu'elle en ait toujours la plus claire conscience, représente aux yeux des historiens, le meilleur de l'âme nationale.

[34] Ned Ward, *The London Spy,* ed. Kenneth Fenwick (London: Folio Society, 1955), p. xi.

[35] Ward, *London Spy,* p. xi.

³⁶ Graham, *The Beginnings of English Literary Periodicals*, p. 39.

³⁷ Ward, *London Spy* (No. 10), p. 175.

³⁸ Graham, *The Beginnings of English Literary Periodicals*, p. 47. Also see Graham's *English Literary Periodicals* (New York: T. Nelson and Sons, 1930), p. 58n.

³⁹ *Observator*, III (1 April 1704).

⁴⁰ It is interesting to note the Observator's reaction on 6 May 1704 to the countryman's report that "some People" did not like the stories related. He spits in their eyes: "Nor do I like those People; our *Laws* and *Liberties* are never the worse because they are Old . . . But I don't write to Please every Body, that task no wife-man would undertake, 'tis an impossibility. I'll tell thee a story. . . ." See the *Observator*, III (3 May 1704).

⁴¹ *Ladies' Diary*, 1706, "The Womens Almanack," pp. [14–15]. Quoted by Mayo, p. 30.

⁴² See Mayo, p. 30. Mayo is mistaken in the listing of the full title in the text, but not in his notes. See also Richmond P. Bond, ed., *Studies in the Early English Periodical* (Chapel Hill: Univ. of North Carolina Press, 1957), p. 42.

⁴³ Mayo, p. 33.

⁴⁴ See especially pp. 150–56. In my discussion of the short fiction in the *Tatler* I am heavily indebted to Richmond P. Bond's conclusions.

⁴⁵ See Mayo, p. 35. Papers on Cynthio (Nos. 1, 5, 22, 35, 58, and 65) and on Jenny and Pacolet and the Upholsterer are examples of the cumulative episode.

⁴⁶ Richmond P. Bond, *The Tatler: The Making of a Literary Periodical* (Cambridge, Mass.: Harvard Univ. Press, 1971), p. 151.

⁴⁷ Richmond P. Bond, *The Tatler*, p. 207.

CHAPTER 2

¹ The "looseness" of approach is plainly stated in Addison's editorial announcement in No. 249: "When I make Choice of a Subject that has not been treated of by others, I throw together my Reflections on it without any Order or Method, so that they may appear rather in the Looseness and Freedom of an Essay, than in the Regularity of a Set Discourse" (*Spectator*, II, 465).

² Steele, in *The Guardian* No. 168, speaks knowledgeably about Theophrastan Characters and uses them as a yardstick by which he measures the value of a Character from *Proverbs*.

³ Benjamin Boyce, *The Theophrastan Character in England to 1642* (Cambridge, Mass.: Harvard Univ. Press, 1947), p. 4.

[4] For an excellent full-length study of Theophrastan influence before 1642 see Boyce, *The Theophrastan Character*, pp. 1–52; also see Edward Chauncey Baldwin, "The Relation of the Seventeenth Century Character to the Periodical Essay," *PMLA*, 19, New Series (1904), 80.

[5] Richard Aldington, ed., *A Book of Characters* (London: G. Routledge and Sons, 1940), p. 6.

[6] Boyce, *The Theophrastan Character*, pp. 5–6.

[7] Boyce, *The Theophrastan Character*, p. 22.

[8] Gwendolen Murphy, ed., *A Cabinet of Characters* (London: Humphrey Milford, Oxford Univ. Press, 1925), p. viii.

[9] In his *Characters of Vertues and Vices* (London, 1608).

[10] See Boyce, *The Theophrastan Character*, p. 123.

[11] Baldwin, "The Relation of the Seventeenth Century Character to the Periodical Essay," p. 89.

[12] Baldwin, "The Relation of the Seventeenth Century Character to the Periodical Essay," p. 98.

[13] Boyce, *The Theophrastan Character*, p. 149. Butler also appears frequently to satirize individuals without giving their names.

[14] The notion that Steele was the one primarily interested in love and domestic issues would be tempered greatly; otherwise, however, Steele and Addison used the same general methods. They *were* Mr. Spectator—fused in approach as a unit.

[15] (Baton Rouge, La.: Louisiana State Univ. Press, 1956), p. 10.

[16] Two valuable studies of La Bruyère's influence on the *Spectator* are E. C. Baldwin's "La Bruyère's Influence upon Addison," *PMLA*, 19, New Series (1904), 479–95, and Margaret Turner's "The Influence of La Bruyère on the 'Tatler' and 'Spectator.'" Baldwin's suggestive but general remarks show that La Bruyère was the "first to combine the features of the Montaigne essay with those of the formal Character," and with "the character-sketch thus individualized and adapted to the uses of the essayist," he says, "both Addison and his colleagues were no doubt perfectly familiar" (pp. 482–83). Turner attempts to reveal more exactly the influence of La Bruyère in a few selected Characters and concludes that we "have not, then, to look for only one kind of character-sketch in the *Tatler* and *Spectator*, but to detect the use of a number of methods derived from La Bruyère" (p. 12). One book of note on the subject, Wilhelm Papenheim's *Die Charakterschilderungen im "Tatler," "Spectator," und "Guardian"* (Leipzig: Bernhard Tauchnitz, 1930), offers a lengthy list of parallels, some of them very broad, which suggest a large debt to Jean de La Bruyère. See Watson, *Magazine Serials*, pp. 10, 91n.

[17] Also note the definition of "Ambition" at the beginning of "The Ambitious Man" (No. 255), *Spectator*, II, 490.

[18] See Boyce, *The Theophrastan Character*, p. 147.

[19] Watson, *Magazine Serials*, p. 11.

[20] See Boyce, *The Theophrastan Character*, p. 180.

[21] See Samuel Butler for a similar technique in "A Modern Politician."

[22] See *Spectator*, I, 332n.

[23] It is interesting to note also that the actions related are not in a seemingly unconnected manner as was true of those following the Theophrastan pattern. For example, notice the connecting transitional phrases "I then applied," "Not long after this," and "I at length studied" (*Spectator*, I, 105).

[24] The letter is signed "Philonous."

[25] The episode between a young fellow and two gentlemen whispering also serves to individualize the type.

[26] Watson, *Magazine Serials*, p. 10.

[27] See Murphy, p. viii; and Chapter 2 of this study, p. 26.

[28] Boyce, *The Theophrastan Character*, p. 19.

CHAPTER 3

[1] Watson, *Magazine Serials*, p. 11.

[2] The story is "The Fable of the Two Owls" from the *Turkish Tales* (Tonson, 1708), pp. 174–76. See *Spectator*, IV, 318n.

[3] Johnson, *Lives of the English Poets*, II, 283.

[4] Watson, *Magazine Serials*, p. 12.

[5] The fable, as Donald F. Bond notes, is from the *Bustan*, or *Garden*, of the Persian poet Sadi. It is quoted in the *Voyages de Chardin* (Amsterdam, 1711), VIII, 19.

[6] These include the following fables, or references to said fables: Addison's "The Ass in the Lion's Skin" (No. 13); Addison's "Of Tongs and Gridiron" (No. 46); Addison's "The Paw of a Lion Rather than the Hoof of an Ass" (No. 61); Steele's "Sedition of Members of the Body" (No. 174); Addison's "Polyphemus" (No. 225); Addison's "The Traveller and the Grasshoppers" (No. 355); Budgell's "Wealth the Father of Love" (No. 506); and Steele's presentation of Dryden's "Cynon and Iphigenia" (No. 71).

[7] Steele probably read it in L'Estrange's *Fables of Aesop* (1692), Fable 240.

[8] See Watson, *Magazine Serials*, p. 12.

CHAPTER 4

[1] Eustace Budgell wrote one dream vision (No. 301); Thomas Parnell helped with two (Nos. 460 and 501); the author of two (Nos. 425 and 524) is undetermined. Addison therefore is the author of eleven (Nos. 3, 56, 63, 83, 159, 275, 281, 463, 464, 499, and 511).

[2] See especially Nos. 3, 63, 463, and 499. See Watson, *Magazine Serials*, p. 10.

[3] See Northrop Frye, *Anatomy of Criticism: Four Essays* (Princeton: Princeton Univ. Press, 1957), p. 90; such allegory he calls "naive."

[4] *Tatler* No. 120 is also a typical earlier example of this method.

[5] Quoted by Donald F. Bond in *Spectator*, I, 240n. Hurd's *The Works of the Right Honourable Joseph Addison* was published in six volumes at London.

[6] Addison's "The Golden Scales" (No. 463), although it does not employ the letter device, is also this typical kind of moral allegory. The moral, however, is drawn more openly than usual at the conclusion: "I shall only add, that upon my awaking I was sorry to find my Golden Scales vanished, but resolved for the future to learn this Lesson from them, not to despise or value any Things for their Appearances, but to regulate my Esteem and Passions towards them according to their real and intrinsick Value" (*Spectator*, IV, 137–38). Parnell's "The Paradise of Fools" (No. 460) and "The Grotto of Grief" (No. 501) are two other socially oriented moral dream visions-cum-allegory that need not be discussed specifically here because the subject matter, method of handling, and fictional techniques are comparable with No. 524 except for the letter device.

[7] William Flint Thrall, Addison Hibbard, and C. Hugh Holman, eds., *A Handbook to Literature*, rev. ed. (New York: The Odyssey Press, 1960), p. 458.

CHAPTER 5

[1] Martha Pike Conant, *The Oriental Tale in England in the Eighteenth Century* (New York: Columbia Univ. Press, 1908), p. xxii.

[2] Galland's twelve-volume *Les Mille et une Nuits, contes arabes* was published in Paris between 1704 and 1717. The 1706 English translation of his French translation (for A. Bell) was of volumes five and six. See *Spectator*, IV, 410n.

[3] Watson, *Magazine Serials*, p. 12.

[4] Conant, pp. xv–xvi.

[5] See Chapters 3 and 4 above, pp. 54–55 and 72–73.

⁶ Conant, p. xxv.

⁷ Conant, pp. 79–80.

⁸ No. 237 does not conform to Conant's definition of oriental material—she excepted Palestine—but it contains obvious orientalisms and deserves treatment here.

⁹ In 1712 the *Histoire des Revolutions de Portugal* by Rene-Aubert de Vertot d'Auboeuf appeared, with an English translation in the same year by John Hughes. Addison follows Hughes's translation. See *Spectator*, III, 301n.

¹⁰ See, for example, Dr. Samuel Johnson's oriental tales in *The Rambler*.

¹¹ Watson, *Magazine Serials*, p. 13.

¹² Conant, p. 84.

¹³ See Conant, pp. 241–42.

CHAPTER 6

¹ Mayo, p. 40.

² Mayo, p. 38.

³ See Walter Francis Wright, *Sensibility in English Prose Fiction, 1760–1814: A Reinterpretation*, University of Illinois Studies in Language and Literature, Nos. 3–4, XXII (Urbana, Ill.: The University of Illinois, 1937), 14.

⁴ Ernest A. Baker, *The History of the English Novel* (New York: Barnes and Noble, 1967), V, 28–29.

⁵ Thrall, Hibbard, and Holman, p. 451.

⁶ Tansy is a pudding or omelet flavored with juice of tansy.

⁷ Thrall, Hibbard, and Holman, p. 197.

⁸ Dunlop, II, 35.

⁹ Donald F. Bond notes: "The story is told in *L'Academie galante* (Paris, 1682), pp. 160–63, and in Bayle, art. Fontevraud, Remark L △ △. Addison's account is fuller, particularly in the details at the end, than either of these two sources." Steele's "Sapphira and Rhynsault" (No. 491) is another story that is taken from Bayle, art. "Burgundy (Charles, Duke of)," Remark N., and it too is rogue literature. In it the treacherous Rhynsault tries to steal Sapphira, another man's wife, and is executed for attempting to do so. The story is highly sentimental and illustrates that justice comes to the wicked libertine in full measure (See *Spectator*, I, 240–44).

¹⁰ Similarly, in No. 375 Hughes relates a rogue story, "Amanda," which has a happy ending that would have delighted most of the *Spectator*'s female readers. The story has a plot similar to Richardson's

Pamela, even in its epistolary techniques (see *Spectator,* III, 409–13).

[11] No source for the story is known.

[12] Steele's "Soldier and Country Girl" (No. 342) is a similar story that contains a fair amount of roguish behavior. A soldier meets and marries a quiet country girl to whom he gives jewels and finery. Narcissus-like, she is consumed by the idea of her own beauty and deserts her husband for the gay life in town (see *Spectator,* III, 269–71).

[13] Mayo, p. 38.

[14] Mayo says that there are "several satirical adventure stories" in the *Spectator,* but he does not elaborate. He is undoubtedly mistaken. See Mayo, p. 38.

[15] See above, p. 76.

[16] Mayo, p. 37.

[17] These narratives contain elements of the domestic apologue but have been discussed previously in the section on the fabliau and rogue literature: "The Castilian and His Wife" (No. 198), "Soldier and Country Girl" (No. 342), and "Amanda" (No. 375).

[18] Note that here Mr. Spectator does not insist upon the truth of his story.

[19] The story is, of course, a retelling of the famous medieval love story of Eloisa and Abelard, which was translated into English in 1713 by Addison and Steele's friend John Hughes. Pope used Hughes's work in the composition of his *Eloisa to Abelard.*

[20] A similar example of the use of a surprise ending is employed in the domestic apologue "Procris and Cephalus" (No. 527), which is included in a letter from a correspondent. Taken from the *Metamorphoses,* the story concerns a tragedy between a husband and wife. Procris, wife of Cephalus, made him an unerring javelin, which caused him to spend much time in the woods. She began to wonder about his affection for seclusion and followed him one day. Mistaking her for a deer when she made a noise, he killed her. This poetic justice is startlingly conveyed in this piece by an unknown author.

[21] These are not the only stories used to point a moral. There are some other instances where very brief (two-or-three-sentence) anecdotes are used to illustrate an argument, but they are not significant enough to be discussed at length. Whether they actually enter the realm of fiction is debatable.

[22] Donald F. Bond notes that the story is taken from Plutarch, "Sayings of Spartans," *Moralia* 235C–235E and Cicero's *De Senectute,* 18.63.

[23] Budgell's "Old Man in Coffee-House" (No. 150) has definite simi-

larities with this exemplum. To illustrate a discussion of poverty, an anecdote is told about an old man who gets bad service in a coffee-house while a fop gets excellent service—but the poorly dressed old man pays the bill for his son, who is the fop.

²⁴ Martyn's two anecdotes from Plutarch's *Life of Pyrrhus,* 21.9–10 and 14:2–7, in *Spectator* No. 180 also illustrate an idea—the vanity of conquests—in an ironical vein. In one, Mr. Spectator communicates a letter from Philarithmus who says, " 'This brings to my Mind a Saying of King *Pyrrhus,* after he had a second Time beat the *Romans* in a pitched Battle, and was complimented by his Generals, *Yes,* says he, *such another Victory and I am quite undone'* " (*Spectator,* II, 211).

²⁵ The story is found, according to Donald F. Bond, in Saint-Evre-mond, "A Letter to the Dutchess of Mazarin," in *Works,* 1714, ii. 131–32 (See *Spectator,* IV, 153*n*).

CHAPTER 7

¹ For an excellent survey of the *Spectator*'s contemporary readers, see Bond's Introduction in *Spectator,* I, lxxxiii–xcvi.

² John Bunn Heidler, *The History, From 1700–1800, of English Criticism of Prose Fiction,* University of Illinois Studies in Language and Literature, No. 2, XIII (Urbana, Ill.: Univ. of Illinois Press, 1928), 23.

³ Stevenson, p. 6.

⁴ Watson, *Magazine Serials,* p. 13.

⁵ Quoted by Heidler, p. 27.

⁶ See Charlotte E. Morgan, *The Rise of the Novel of Manners: A Study of English Prose Fiction Between 1600 to 1740* (New York: Columbia Univ. Press, 1911), p. 95, for an estimate of how much the *Spectator* influenced the novel of manners and Mayo and Watson for information concerning the nature of periodical fiction after the *Spectator.*

Select Bibliography

Addison, Joseph, Sir Richard Steele, and others. *The Spectator.* Ed. Gregory Smith. 4 vols. London: J. M. Dent, 1961, and New York: E. P. Dutton, 1961.

————. *The Spectator.* Ed Donald F. Bond. 5 vols. Oxford: The Clarendon Press, 1965.

Aitken, George A. *The Life of Richard Steele.* 2 vols. Boston and New York: Houghton Mifflin Co., 1889.

Aldington, Richard, ed. and trans. *A Book of Characters.* London: G. Routledge and Sons, 1940.

Altenbernd, Lynn, and Leslie L. Lewis, eds. *Introduction to Literature: Stories.* New York: Macmillan Co., 1963.

Athenian Oracle. Publication of the Athenian Society. 4 vols. London: The Athenian Society, 1703–10.

Baldwin, Edward C. "The Relation of the Seventeenth Century Character to the Periodical Essay." *PMLA,* 19 (1904), 75–114.

————. "La Bruyère's Influence Upon Addison." *PMLA,* 19 (1904), 479–95.

Beachcroft, T. O. *The English Short Story.* Writers and Their Work Series, Nos. 168–69. London: Longmans, Green and Co., 1964.

Bennett, Edwin Keppel. *A History of the German Novelle.* Cambridge: Cambridge Univ. Press, 1961.

Blair, Hugh. *Lectures on Rhetoric and Belles Lettres.* 2 vols. London, 1783.

Blanchard, Rae. "Richard Steele's Maryland Story." *American Quarterly,* 10 (1958), 78–82.

Bond, Donald F. "The First Printing of the *Spectator.*" *Modern Philology,* 47 (1950), 164–77.

————. "The Text of the *Spectator.*" *Studies in Bibliography,* 5 (1953), 109–28.

————. "Addison in Perspective." *Modern Philology,* 54 (1956), 124–28.

Bond, Richmond P. "Eighteenth Century Correspondence: A Survey." *Studies in Philology*, 33 (1936), 572-86.

———. "The Business of the *Spectator*." *University of North Carolina Extension Bulletin*, No. 3, 32 (1953), 7-20.

———, ed. *Studies in the Early English Periodical*. Chapel Hill: Univ. of North Carolina Press, 1957.

———, ed. *New Letters to the 'Tatler' and 'Spectator.'* Austin: Univ. of Texas Press, 1959.

———. *The Tatler: The Making of a Literary Periodical*. Cambridge, Mass.: Harvard Univ. Press, 1971.

Booth, Wayne C. "The Self-Conscious Narrator in Comic Fiction Before *Tristram Shandy*." *PMLA*, 67 (1952), 163-85.

———. *The Rhetoric of Fiction*. Chicago: Univ. of Chicago Press, 1961.

Boyce, Benjamin. "English Short Fiction in the Eighteenth Century: A Preliminary View." *Studies in Short Fiction*, 5 (Winter 1968), 95-112.

———. *The Theophrastan Character in England to 1642*. Cambridge, Mass: Harvard Univ. Press, 1947.

Bredvold, Louis I. *The Natural History of Sensibility*. Detroit: Wayne State Univ. Press, 1962.

British Apollo. 4 vols. London, 13 Feb. 1708-11 May 1711.

Brooks, Cleanth, and Robert Penn Warren. *The Scope of Fiction*. New York: Appleton-Century-Crofts, 1960.

Bryan, William F., and R. S. Crane, eds. *The English Familiar Essay*. Boston: Ginn and Co., 1916.

Canby, Henry Seidel. *The Short Story in English*. New York: Henry Holt and Co., 1909.

Chambers, Robert D. "Addison at Work on the *Spectator*." *Modern Philology*, 56 (1959), 145-53.

Chandler, Zilpha E. *An Analysis of the Stylistic Technique of Addison, Johnson, Hazlitt, and Pater*. Iowa City: Univ. of Iowa Press, 1928.

Conant, Martha Pike. *The Oriental Tale in England in the Eighteenth Century*. New York: Columbia Univ. Press, 1908.

Connely, Willard. *Sir Richard Steele*. New York: Charles Scribner's Sons, 1934.

Cooke, Arthur L. "Addison vs. Steele, 1708." *PMLA*, 68 (1953), 313–20.

Cross, Ethan Allen. *A Book of the Short Story*. New York: American Book Co., 1934.

Cross, Wilbur L. *The Development of the English Novel*. New York: Macmillan Co., 1899.

Cuff, Roger Penn, ed. *An American Short Story Survey*. Harrisburg, Pa.: Stackpole Co., 1953.

Cunningham, Robert Newton. *Peter Anthony Motteux, 1663–1718*. Oxford: B. Blackwell, 1933.

de la Roche, Michael, ed. *Memoirs of Literature*. 4 vols. London, 13 March 1710–6 Sept. 1714.

Dobrée, Bonamy. *English Essayists*. London: Collins, 1946.

———. *English Literature in the Early Eighteenth Century, 1700–1740*. Oxford: The Clarendon Press, 1959.

Dobson, Austin. *Richard Steele*. London: Longmans, Green and Co., 1888.

———. *Side-walk Studies*. London: H. Milford, Oxford Univ. Press, 1924.

Dunlop, John Colin. *History of Prose Fiction*. Rev. Henry Wilson. 2 vols. London: George Bell & Sons, 1986.

Dunton, John, ed. *The Athenian Gazette; or, Casuistical Mercury*. London, 17 March 1691–14 June 1697.

Elioseff, Lee Andrew. *The Cultural Milieu of Addison's Literary Criticism*. Austin: Univ. of Texas Press, 1963.

Esdaile, Arundell. *A List of English Tales and Prose Romances Printed Before 1740*. London: The Bibliographical Society by Blades, East, & Blades, 1912.

Foster, Dorothy. "The Earliest Precursor of Our Present-Day Monthly Miscellanies." *PMLA*, 25, New Series (1917), 22–58.

Freeman, Phyllis. "Who Was Sir Roger de Coverley?" *Quarterly Review*, 285 (1947), 592–604.

Gay, John. *The Present State of Wit (1711)*. Augustan Reprint Society, 1st series, No. 3. Ann Arbor: Edwards Brothers, 1947.

Gerhardt, Mia I. *The Art of Story-Telling: A Literary Study of The Thousand and One Nights*. Leiden: E. J. Brill, 1963.

Glicksberg, Charles I. *Writing the Short Story.* New York: Hendricks House, 1953.

Gordon, R. C., ed. *The Expanded Moment: A Short Story Anthology.* Boston: D. C. Heath & Co., 1963.

Gove, Philip Babcock. *The Imaginary Voyage in Prose Fiction.* New York: Columbia Univ. Press, 1941.

Graham, Walter James. *The Beginnings of English Literary Periodicals: A Study of Periodical Literature, 1665–1715.* New York: Oxford Univ. Press, 1926.

———. *English Literary Periodicals.* New York: T. Nelson and Sons, 1930.

Greenough, Chester N. *A Bibliography of the Theophrastan Character in English.* Cambridge, Mass.: Harvard Univ. Press, 1947.

Hall, James B., and Joseph Langland, eds. *The Short Story.* New York: Macmillan Co., 1956.

Heidler, Joseph Bunn. *The History, From 1700 to 1800, of English Criticism of Prose Fiction.* University of Illinois Studies in Language and Literature. Urbana: Univ. of Illinois Press, 1928. XIII, No. 2, 1–187.

Hughes, Helen Sard. "English Epistolary Fiction before 'Pamela.'" *The Manly Anniversary Studies.* Chicago, 1923. Pp. 156–69.

Humphreys, A. R. *Steele, Addison and Their Periodical Essays.* Writers and Their Work Series, No. 109. London: Longmans, Green and Co., 1959.

Ito, Hiroyuki. "The Language of *The Spectator*—Chiefly concerning the Aspect of Double Meaning." *Anglica* (Publication of The Anglica Society of Kansai University, Osaka, Japan), 5 (1962), 36–62.

Irving, Washington. *Letters of Washington Irving to Henry Brevoort.* Ed. George S. Hellman. New York: G. P. Putnam's Sons, 1918.

Jones, Silas Paul. *A List of French Prose Fiction from 1700 to 1750.* New York: The H. W. Wilson Co., 1939.

Kaye, F. B., and R. S. Crane. *A Census of British Newspapers and Periodicals, 1620–1800.* Chapel Hill: Univ. of North Carolina Press, 1927.

Kempton, Kenneth Payson. *The Short Story.* Cambridge, Mass.: Harvard Univ. Press, 1947.

Kenney, William. "The Morality of the *Spectator.*" *Notes and Queries,* 4 (1957), 37–38.

Kitchin, George W. *Sir Roger L'Estrange: A Contribution to the History of the Press in the Seventeenth Century.* N.p., 1913.

Lannering, Jan. *Studies in the Prose Style of Joseph Addison.* Upsala Essays and Studies on Language and Literature. Upsala: Lundequist, 1951. IX, 1–203.

Liddell, Robert. *Some Principles of Fiction.* London: J. Cape, 1953.

Lillie, Charles, ed. *Original and Genuine Letters Sent to the Tatler and Spectator.* 2 vols. London, 1725.

McBurney, W. H. *A Check List of English Prose Fiction, 1700–1739.* Cambridge, Mass.: Harvard Univ. Press, 1960.

Marr, George S. *The Periodical Essayists of the Eighteenth Century.* New York: Appleton and Co., 1924.

Matthews, Brander. *The Short Story.* New York: American Book Co., 1907.

Matthews, W. "The Character-Writings of Edward Ward." *Neophilologus,* 21 (1936), 116–34.

Mayo, Robert D. *The English Novel in the Magazines, 1740–1815.* Evanston, Ill.: Northwestern Univ. Press, 1962.

Millar, J. H. *The Mid-Eighteenth Century.* New York: Charles Scribner's Sons, 1902.

Mish, Charles C., ed. *Short Fiction of the Seventeenth Century.* New York: New York Univ. Press, 1963.

Morgan, Charlotte E. *The Rise of the Novel of Manners: A Study of English Prose Fiction Between 1600 to 1740.* New York: Columbia Univ. Press, 1911.

Motteux, Peter Anthony, ed. *Gentleman's Journal; or, The Monthly Miscellany.* 2 vols. London, Jan. 1962–Nov. 1694.

Murphy, Gwendolen. *A Cabinet of Characters.* London: Humphrey Milford, Oxford Univ. Press, 1925.

———. *A Bibliography of English Character-books, 1608–1700.* Oxford Univ. Press for the Bibliographical Society, 1925.

Newman, Frances. *The Short Story's Mutations from Petronius to*

Paul Morand. New York: B. W. Huebsch, 1924.

O'Brien, Edward J., ed. *Elizabethan Tales.* London: George Allen & Unwin, 1937.

Observator. 11 vols. London, 1702–12.

O'Connor, Frank. *The Lonely Voice: A Study of the Short Story.* Cleveland and New York: The World Publishing Co., 1963.

Papenheim, Wilhelm. *Die Charakterschilderungen im 'Tatler,' 'Spectator,' und 'Guardian.'* Leipzig: Bernhard Tauchnitz, 1930.

Peden, William. *The American Short Story.* Boston: Houghton Mifflin Co., 1964.

Rau, Fritz. "Texte, Ausgaben und Verfasser des *Tatler* und *Spectator.* Forschungsbericht." *Germanisch-Romanische Monatsschrift, Neue Folge,* 8 (1958), 126–44.

Read, Herbert. *English Prose Style.* Boston: Beacon Press, 1952.

Ross, Danforth. *The American Short Story.* University of Minnesota Pamphlets on American Writers, No. 14. Minneapolis: Univ. of Minnesota Press, 1961.

Schlauch, Margaret. "English Short Fiction in the 15th and 16th Centuries." *Studies in Short Fiction,* 3 (1966), 393–434.

Sherbo, Arthur. *English Sentimental Drama.* East Lansing, Mich.: Michigan State Univ. Press, 1957.

Simpson, Donald Roberts. *The Spectator Reconsidered.* Ann Argor, Mich.: University Microfilms, 1962. Diss. University of Colorado, 1962.

Singer, Godfrey F. *The Epistolary Novel.* Philadelphia: Univ. of Pennsylvania Press, 1933.

Smithers, Peter. *Life of Joseph Addison.* Oxford: The Clarendon Press, 1954.

Stephens, John C., Jr. "Addison and Steele's 'Spectator.'" *Times Literary Supplement,* 15 Dec. 1950, p. 801.

Stevenson, Lionel. *The English Novel: A Panorama.* Boston: Houghton Mifflin Co., 1960.

Swayne, George C. *Herodotus.* Philadelphia: J. B. Lippincott & Co., 1875.

Thomson, J. A. K. *Classical Influences on English Prose.* London: George Allen & Unwin, 1956.

Thorpe, Clarence DeWitt. "Addison and Some of His Predecessors on 'Novelty.'" *PMLA*, 52 (1937), 1114–29.

Thrall, William F., Addison Hibbard, and C. Hugh Holman. *A Handbook to Literature*. Rev. ed. New York: The Odyssey Press, 1960.

Turner, Margaret. "The Influence of La Bruyère on the 'Tatler' and the 'Spectator.'" *Modern Language Review*, 48 (1953), 10–16.

Ward, Ned. *The London Spy*, ed. Kenneth Fenwick. London: Folio Society, 1955.

Watson, Melvin R. *Magazine Serials and the Essay Tradition, 1746–1820*. Louisiana State University Studies, Humanities Series, No. 6. Baton Rouge: Louisiana State Univ. Press, 1956.

———. "The *Spectator* Tradition and the Development of the Familiar Essay." *ELH*, 13 (1946), 189–215.

Watt, Ian P. *The Rise of the Novel*. Berkeley: Univ. of California Press, 1959.

West, Ray B., Jr. *The Short Story in America, 1900–1950*. Freeport, New York: Books for Libraries Press, 1952.

West, Ray B., Jr. and Robert W. Stallman, eds. *The Art of Modern Fiction*. New York: Holt, Rinehart & Winston, 1949.

Wheeler, William. *A Concordance to the Spectator*. London, 1897.

Wieder, Robert. *Pierre Motteux et les Debuts du Journalisme en Angleterre au XVII siècle: Le Gentleman's Journal (1692–1694)*. Paris, n.d.

Wiles, Roy McKeen. *Serial Publication in England before 1750*. Cambridge: Cambridge Univ. Press, 1957.

Winton, Calhoun. *Captain Steele: The Early Career of Richard Steele*. Baltimore, Md.: Johns Hopkins Univ. Press, 1964.

———. *Sir Richard Steele, M.P.: The Later Career*. Baltimore, Md.: Johns Hopkins Univ. Press, 1970.

Wolley, Richard, ed. [for John Dunton]. *Compleat Library*, or *News for the Ingenius*. London, May 1692–April 1694.

Wood, Frederick T. Review of Wilhelm Papenheim, *Die Charakterschilderungen im 'Tatler,' 'Spectator,' und 'Guardian'* (Leipzig: Bernhard Tauchnitz, 1930). *English Studies*, 15 (1933), 198–200.

Index